PUMPKIN SPICED POSSIBILITIES

Samantha Baca

Stone Creek Series

Chocolate Covered Mistletoe

Candy Coated Promises

Pumpkin Spiced Possibilites

Cover Design: Richard Baca
Image(s): Canva

Contents

One	1
Two	3
Three	9
Four	19
Five	25
Six	35
Seven	39
Eight	49
Nine	53
Ten	61
Eleven	69
Twelve	75
Thirteen	87
Fourteen	99
Fifteen	105
Sixteen	111
Seventeen	123
Eighteen	129
Nineteen	137
Twenty	143
Twenty One	149
Twenty Two	153
Twenty Three	165
Twenty Four	169
Epilogue	175
Other Books By Samantha Baca	185
Acknowledgements	189
About the Author	191

<u>One</u>

Gen

"Shh, don't talk, mama," I whispered as the tear escaped and slid down my cheek. I squeezed her hand gently, afraid to hurt her.

"Just listen to me," she said, her voice quiet and raspy as she struggled to get the words out. "I love you more than you'll ever know. Don't be afraid to live life and be happy."

I sucked in a deep breath and forced myself to hold it. Now wasn't the time to break down and cry. She needed me to be strong for her, even in her last minutes. The doctor had confirmed that she would pass soon, and I was holding onto every second that I had with her.

"Live your life," she whispered again, squeezing my hand with the little strength that she had left. "I just want you to be happy."

"Okay, mama," I agreed, the tears flowing freely as she closed her eyes and relaxed against the pillow. With one last breath, she was gone.

I heard people moving around me as my step-dad, Sean, talked to the doctor on the phone, confirming that she had passed. I debated whether to go find my siblings and make sure they were okay. Instead, I felt numb as I sat there, staring at her.

She was beautiful. Every tiny detail about her that I had taken for granted all of these years was now staring me in the face, as I tried to freeze them in my memory so I would never forget her. Like the small scar just above her eyebrow from where she had pierced it as an act of rebellion against her parents when she was sixteen, or the way her lips turned up in the corners whenever she was trying to be serious but found something to be funny and couldn't keep a straight face.

I held onto her hand, afraid to let go for the last time. I allowed myself to fall into the grief that was ready to consume me, as I thought about her last words to me.

Don't be afraid to live life and be happy.

Two

Gen- 2 Months Later

I drove with the radio blaring, drowning out the silence, as I made my way to Stone Creek, Tennessee. I hadn't been back here since my mom had taken a turn for the worst in September. She had been sick for a while, then all of a sudden, something changed, and she went from okay to terminal within a week. I'd spent all of my time by her side, desperate for any time with her.

After losing my mom, everything around me started to spiral out of control. So many things had changed that I was left with nothing that felt normal anymore. Sean decided to move to Alabama with the kids to be closer to his family and offered for me to come with them. While I wasn't opposed to moving and starting over, there was something inside of me that said that Alabama wasn't the place for me.

I had talked to my dad, Parker, several times over the past few months, and despite his numerous attempts to convince me to *move* back to Tennessee, I gave in and agreed to come *visit* for Thanksgiving. Not that I had much to feel thankful about these days. I had spiraled into a depression so dark that even Darth Vader looked like a bright ray of sunshine.

The last time I was in Stone Creek, I had spent so much time with his girlfriend, Sheila and her kids, that it actually felt like being with family, which was what I needed right now. It wasn't that I didn't love Sean, my step-dad and siblings, I just didn't feel like going to Alabama and dealing with people asking us how we were doing and talking about my mom when they barely even knew her. Sheila and Parker were the perfect combination of being around family without having the loss of my mom shoved in my face at every turn. And if all else failed, I could always count on Brooke, Sheila's best friend, to bring wine and help me forget whatever I needed to.

The speed limit decreased, as I took the exit I needed and headed to their house. It still felt weird to say that I was going to my dad's house for the holidays, yet here I was.

I parked and got out, grabbing my duffle bag from the seat next to me. I slung it over my shoulder and tucked my phone into my pocket, as I looked at the house. I pulled in a deep breath and reminded myself that I could do this. There was no reason to break down and cry. I was strong, and today was supposed to be a fun day.

"Gen!" Sally yelled, flinging the door open as she ran out to meet me at my car.

"Hey," I laughed, wrapping my arms around her. "Did you get taller?" I asked, looking down to see her face.

"My mama says that I'm growing like a weed," she laughed. "But I'm sure that I'll slow down some, now that I'm thirteen."

I laughed with her, as we walked up to the house. I felt terrible that I had missed her birthday this summer and made sure to bring a gift with me to make up for it. She opened the door, and the smell of turkey and fresh-baked bread floated out, making my stomach growl.

We went inside and closed the door behind us. I set my bag down on the floor beside the couch so it was out of the way.

"Hey," Parker said as he walked out of the kitchen and saw me. "You made it!"

"Hi, Dad," I replied against his chest as he hugged me tightly.

I expected him to say something about losing my mom, but I was thankful that he didn't. Sheila had called me right after it happened when she couldn't come to the funeral with Parker. They had both been incredibly supportive, and I couldn't thank them enough for everything they had done for us. From the beautiful flower arrangement they had at her service, to the trays of desserts that Brooke and Ryder sent with my dad, they all went above and beyond.

"I hope you're hungry," he teased, pulling back to look at me. "Sheila and Brooke have been cooking up a storm in there. We should be ready to eat soon."

I looked around, remembering the time that I had spent here with Sheila last year. No one could find my dad, and we didn't know that he had been in a terrible car accident.

I said quick hellos to the kids, smiling when I saw the scowling look on Parker's face as Megan introduced me to her new boyfriend. Oliver had his longtime girlfriend there too, but it didn't seem to bother Parker as much as it did that his *daughter* had a boyfriend. For a moment, I was thankful that he got to miss out on that part of my life. Lord knew that I sure gave my momma a load of trouble with the guys that I brought home, and ninety percent of Sean's grey hair was from my teenage years.

"Something smells delicious in here," I said happily as I walked into the kitchen and wrapped my arm around Sheila's shoulders.

"Hey, sweetie!" She turned her head and planted a quick kiss on my cheek, before turning her attention back to the pot of gravy that she was thickening.

"Hi, Brooke," I said, giving her a quick hug in between her transferring dishes from the oven to the table. "Can I help with anything?"

"You have perfect timing," Brooke joked, tossing me a set of oven mitts. "Can you grab the green bean casserole from the oven for me?"

She rearranged a few things on the table that was already packed with food and smiled, pleased with herself.

"It's great to see you, I'm glad you came down to have Thanksgiving with us." She waited for me to set the casserole down on the trivet that she left for me before giving me a real hug.

Sheila finished with the gravy, scooping it into a white gravy boat and setting it on the table before wiping her hands on the apron she was wearing.

"I think we have everything," she sighed. "Am I forgetting anything?"

I looked at the table, unable to think of a single that could be missing.

"It looks complete to me," I laughed, my stomach growling with anticipation as my mouth started to water.

"Well then, let's eat!" She patted my back and pointed to the turkey-shaped name tags that were arranged on the table. I found my name and smiled, knowing that Sally was responsible for this when I found myself sitting between her and Parker.

I washed my hands and took my seat as everyone started piling in. The noise in the small room got loud quickly, but at that moment, I felt like things were normal again for the first time in a long time.

Three

Gen

"Can you pass the mashed potatoes?" Thomas asked over the noise of everyone else talking. I reached over and grabbed the bowl, passing it his way.

There was more food than I knew what to do with, but I piled it on my plate, ready to eat my feelings away. I kept my head down, pushing my food around with my fork, as I tried to make room while Parker opened a bottle of wine.

Once everyone was settled, Sheila said a quick prayer before we started eating. I tucked a strand of hair behind my ear, making sure it didn't get in the way when I realized how hungry I was.

"Wine?" Parker asked, lifting the bottle over an empty glass for me.

"Sure," I smiled, taking the glass when he was finished.

"Sheila?" he offered, nodding to her empty glass.

"No, thank you," she said quietly, keeping her head down as she poked at her turkey with her fork.

"Since when do you not want wine?" Brooke teased, lifting her glass to take a sip. "The only time I've ever known you to say no to a glass of wine during the holidays was when you were—"

I watched as Sheila's face went pale before it quickly turned as red as her fiery locks that framed her face.

"Oh my God!" Brooke gasped, covering her mouth as she set her glass down in front of her. "Are you?"

I glanced over at Parker, who looked like he was in shock, his mouth hanging slightly open as he held the bottle of wine in the air.

"I don't know," she snapped, glaring at Brooke. "Not that it's anyone's business, but yes, I'm late."

"Sheila—" Parker stuttered, not sure what to say.

"Please don't start freaking out," she begged, turning to him. "This is why I haven't said anything yet. I was planning to take a test first, I just haven't had time to go get one."

"There's some in the bathroom, mommy," Sally said happily beside me.

Sheila looked at her with her brows pulled together in confusion.

"I think you might be mistaken, honey," Sheila said sweetly. Sally was her youngest child, but being thirteen, there was a chance she knew what she was talking about. "You must be talking about something else."

"No, it's a pregnancy test."

"How do you know what they look like?" Oliver asked, a look of bewilderment on his face. He was the oldest and I had quickly learned that he was overly protective of his mother and siblings in the short time that I had known him.

"Because there's a picture of them on the box that was in the cabinet under the sink. And then there was a test in the trashcan, with the two pink lines and everything," Sally informed him.

I looked around and waited as the tension mounted in the room.

"Brooke? Are you pregnant?" Sheila asked, turning her attention back to her best friend.

Ryder's face turned beet red as he choked on the piece of bread roll that he had popped into his mouth a few seconds before. He coughed and thumped his chest with his fist to try to dislodge it.

"Calm down, Ryder," Brooke said, reaching over to pat his back. "I'm not pregnant. *You* don't have to freak out."

"Well, then why is there a positive pregnancy test in the—"

Sheila's voice fell when we all heard a sniffle from the other end of the table.

"I'm so sorry, mama. We didn't mean for it to happen," Megan whispered, tears rushing down her face. Her boyfriend, Zach, sat next to her, his head bowed to avoid looking at everyone.

I dropped my fork to my plate, too caught up in the drama that was unfolding in front of me to be able to eat.

Everyone sat there in silence for a few minutes, unsure of what to say.

"I'm going to go get another bottle of wine," Ryder said, excusing himself from the table.

"Where are you going?" Brooke asked as he rushed out of the kitchen, grabbed his jacket, and bolted out the front door.

"Remind me not to miss my birth control," she muttered under her breath as she leaned back against her chair and took a long sip of wine.

"Well," Sheila said, clearing her throat. Both hands were planted firmly beside her plate as if she was struggling to control herself. "This is certainly a surprising turn of events. Nonetheless, today is a day to count our blessings, so let's focus on what we have and enjoy the company of those who have joined us."

She relaxed in her seat for a moment before adding, "Megan, Zack—we'll discuss this after dinner."

Everyone began eating quietly, the only sound in the room was the scraping of forks against the empty plates. I wasn't sure if everyone was so hungry that they devoured every last bite of food, or if they were desperate to occupy their mouths so they didn't have to talk to fill the awkward silence that was lingering in the room.

Ten minutes later, I was helping Sheila clean up while Parker and Brooke sat with the kids in the living room.

"So," she said heavily, dropping a handful of forks into the sink filled with hot, soapy water. "How are you doing?"

"That's a loaded question," I laughed, knowing that either way, whatever conversation we had was going to be a heavy one. "I'm trying to keep myself busy and figure out what to do next."

"I'm really sorry about your mom," she said softly, gently squeezing my shoulder as she turned to grab a stack of plates from the table.

"You can set them there, and I'll wash them," I offered, my hands busy washing the silver wear at the bottom of the sink.

"Na, we'll just rinse them off real quick and toss them in the dishwasher. I only wash the forks because we don't have enough for dinner and dessert, and we can't be missing out on dessert!"

"That would be a sin," I teased, laughing along with her.

"Whew, don't even get me started on that topic," she muttered, adding another stack of dishes and setting them on the counter by the dishwasher.

At that moment, Ryder came back and set two bags down on the counter.

"What's that?" she asked, nodding to them.

"Wine." He shrugged.

She raised a brow and rested her hand on her hip.

"And chocolate. And maybe a few boxes of pregnancy tests. I didn't know who all needed them, so I just bought everything they had."

She walked over and opened the bags, gasping when she looked inside. She pulled two bottles of wine out of one bag, along with two giant bags of assorted mini candy bars. I held back my laughter as I watched her pick up the other bag and dump it on the table, filled with boxes and boxes of pregnancy tests.

"Ryder!" she scolded. "There's at least two hundred dollars worth of pregnancy tests in here!"

"I just wanted everyone to be sure," he said sheepishly, raising his hands in the air. "I think the lady felt bad for me, so she gave me her employee discount, so technically, a handful of those were free."

I turned my head and burst into laughter, no longer able to contain it. Sheila joined in with me as I tried to hide my face with a soap bubble-covered hand.

"I'm just gonna take this in there," he said, grabbing his food from the counter. "Make sure to take the test soon, and maybe have Brooke take a few too?"

"Oh my God," she laughed. "You're worse than a kid."

"Just one or two—you know, make sure my super sperm haven't made their way in yet. It seems to be in the air."

"Pregnancy isn't contagious," Brooke whined, walking in and joining us in the kitchen. She stopped dead in her tracks. Her long, chestnut-colored hair was pulled back into a ponytail, showing the icy blues of her eyes as she caught sight of the table. "Did you buy the whole damn store?" she asked, folding her arms over her chest as she turned to look at him.

"Yes," he nodded quickly. "There are a few boxes in there for you."

He ducked out of her way in time to miss her smacking him, before he darted into the living room with his food.

We all stood there, staring at the table of sin: wine, chocolate, and a year's supply of pregnancy tests.

"Well, what are you waiting for?" Brooke asked, jerking her head toward the table. "Have the kids finish cleaning up, and we'll go take a few and see what they say."

I turned around to give them some privacy, suddenly feeling out of place being there. Being twenty-two, I didn't feel like I fit in with anyone. I was much older than any of the kids and more than ten years younger than them. I turned the water on and started rinsing the forks.

"What are you doing?" Sheila asked, walking over to stand beside me. I turned and looked between her and Brooke. They were both watching me and waiting.

"Rinsing the soap off of the forks?" I replied stupidly.

"Leave them. The kids will do it. I'm sure Megan would *love* to come do some chores," Sheila said sarcastically. "Come on, you're coming with us."

"Grab a bag of chocolate and a bottle of wine," Brooke instructed before walking down the hallway with her arms full. Sheila grabbed the bag from the table and tossed all of the tests back inside before yelling for the kids to finish the dishes.

We went into her bedroom and closed the door. Brooke sat down on the bed and nodded for me to join her as she twisted the cap off of the bottle of wine.

"Ryder knows that I get too impatient to deal with opening the bottle, so he gets me the sweet ones that have a twist-off top," she exerted as she twisted it open.

Sheila was standing in the middle of the room, staring into the bag in her hands.

"Just grab one and go," Brooke suggested, taking a drink directly from the bottle.

"How did I even get here?" Sheila muttered, still looking at the tests. "I'm a mother of *four* teenagers. I'm too old to have another."

"You don't know for sure that you're pregnant. So go take the test, then we can either freak out about it or laugh about it while drinking wine and eating chocolate."

"Fine," she sighed, taking the bag with her into the bathroom.

Brooke opened one of the bags of chocolate and set it on the bed between us. I reached in and grabbed a few, making myself busy while we waited. I don't know who was more anxious about it—her or me.

Five minutes passed without any word from Sheila, and I started to get worried.

"Son of a bitch!" she exclaimed loudly on the other side.

Brooke and I looked at each other and then burst into laughter.

The door flew open, and a bewildered Sheila emerged. She held two pregnancy tests, one in each hand, with her brows shooting clear up to her forehead.

"How did this happen?!" she asked, walking over and holding them out for us to see. Both had a very solid, very definitive positive line on each test.

"Well, I think we all know how this happened," Brooke teased, earning a dirty look from Sheila.

"It's not funny—I'm old enough to be a grandma."

She gasped the moment she said it.

"Oh my God! I *am* going to be a grandma! A *pregnant grandma*!" She plopped down on the bed between us, letting her head fall as she cried.

"Hey, it's going to be okay," I said softly, squeezing her shoulder gently, as she had done for me earlier. "You'll see."

"She's right," Brooke assured her. "It'll all be alright. You've got all of us to help you and Megan through this. That's what family is for."

I felt an odd flutter in my stomach when Brooke said it, but she was right—we were family. From the moment I walked into the house this afternoon, I felt like I was home, like I belonged. And that was a feeling that I was desperate to hold onto for as long as I could.

Four

Gen

"Thanks for coming with us," Sheila said as we got out of the car and headed toward the clinic. I had initially planned to head back home after the holiday but then realized that there was nothing to rush back for. I hadn't been working while my mom was sick and couldn't bring myself to find a job after she died. I knew that I would have to find something sooner rather than later, but my grief assured me that there was plenty of time.

"No problem," I replied, smiling over at Megan, who looked terrified to be here. Sheila had scheduled appointments for them first thing Friday morning and was lucky to get back-to-back spots Monday morning. I guess it was just part of being in a small town where people weren't flocking to the gynecologist's office first thing after Thanksgiving.

"I'm kinda glad that Parker had to work this morning and couldn't make it," Sheila admitted with a laugh as she held the door open for Megan and me. "He's been more freaked out about it than Ryder was, but only because he's worried about whether the baby is okay. I need to see the doctor first, *without* having to babysit him right now."

She laughed, and I knew that she was kidding but that there was also plenty of truth to it. I had seen how shocked he was by the news, followed by the instant fear that she should be sitting down and resting, offering her water every twenty minutes to make sure the baby had enough liquid to swim around in. He and Ryder were peculiar little creatures when it came to pregnancy, but both for different reasons. While Parker was excited to be having a baby, Ryder was still checking in every few minutes to see if Brooke should take a test—just in case she caught it.

We sat down in the lobby and waited. I couldn't imagine that it would be long, given no one else was here and the parking lot was nearly empty when we parked. Ten minutes later, an older nurse with wiry grey hair escorted us back to the exam room and showed them the gowns they needed to put on after they decided who was going first.

I turned to give them privacy as Sheila helped Megan get situated. A few minutes later, there was a knock on the door before it opened, and the most gorgeous-looking specimen of man walked into the room.

I must have swallowed loud enough for everyone to hear me, because he turned and looked, his brow raised in concern. Suddenly, my mouth was as dry as cotton, and I wished that I was invisible, as his charcoal grey eyes studied me.

It felt like minutes had passed with us staring at each other before he turned his attention to Megan and Sheila.

"Hello, ladies," he said, extending his hand to shake theirs before turning back to reach for mine. "I'm Doctor Hayes. I see in your file that you're both here for an ultrasound to date your pregnancy—is that correct?"

"Yes," Sheila confirmed, looking at Megan with a tight smile. "My daughter, Megan, will be going first."

"Sounds good," he said, setting the folder down on the counter behind him. I turned away, giving them privacy as he started the ultrasound.

"Okay, everything looks good so far," he replied quietly, more to himself than anything. "Right here is your baby, and here is its heartbeat."

I turned to the screen in time to see the tiny tadpole-looking fetus he was pointing to before he reached over and turned the speaker up. The quick sound of a heartbeat echoed through the room, bringing tears to Sheila's eyes as she reached down and held Megan's hand. They both started crying, and I felt myself getting emotional, knowing that I would never have this experience with my mom.

I tried to push the pain of jealousy aside and focus on the moment.

"It looks like you're around eight weeks, and based on the date of your last known period, I would say that you're due around July 10th."

"Oh my God," Sheila whispered, leaning down to kiss Megan's forehead. "I'm really going to be a grandma."

"Congratulations," he said, printing the ultrasound pictures after putting the wand away. He reached over and handed them to Megan.

"I'll let you get changed, and then I'll be back to do the next one." He looked directly at me as if he assumed that I was his next patient.

"Oh no, I'm not pregnant," I rushed out, holding my hands up in front of me.

"It's me," Sheila laughed. "I'm apparently a pregnant grandma—which is something that I would have never imagined I would ever say in my life."

"Sorry," he apologized, his eyes quickly traveling the length of my body before looking back at Sheila. "I'll let you get changed, and I'll be back in a few minutes."

He walked out and closed the door behind him. I let out the breath that I hadn't realized I was holding. *What in the world was that?* I felt so jolted by him that I hadn't heard Sheila talking to me.

"Gen? Are you okay?" she asked.

"Me? Yeah, why?" I turned to find her and Megan watching me, curiosity plastered across their faces.

"No reason," Megan replied with a giggle as she finished getting dressed.

"He's cute," Sheila noted with a nod toward the door as she stood beside the table. Before I could answer, there was another knock on the door as he came in to get the exam table ready for Sheila.

I was thankful for the distraction, so I didn't have to answer her. But she was right, he was cute.

Twenty minutes later, we headed out of the clinic with two hormonal pregnant women who now shared the same due date. They laughed, then cried, then laughed some more about the irony of it all. But as we left, all I could think about was the cute doctor who had gotten me so flustered that suddenly I found myself wanting to stick around in Stone Creek for a little while longer.

Five

Gen

"You're *eight* weeks pregnant?!" Brooke exclaimed as we sat down at the high-top table by the window. "How did you not know you were pregnant before then?"

"I don't know," Sheila sighed. "I guess I just assumed that since I was on birth control and thirty-five years old, that it was more likely to be menopause than anything else."

"You just turned thirty-six," Megan countered, picking at the paper straw wrapper in front of her.

"That's enough out of you," Sheila warned, narrowing her eyes. Even I had been in the family long enough to read the playful tone of it. Sheila vehemently denied that she had turned a year older after celebrating my dad's fortieth birthday this summer.

"How are you feeling, Megan?" Brooke asked, turning our attention to her.

"Um, fine, I guess."

"Did you know that you were pregnant before your mom found out that she was?"

Her face went pale quickly as she continued to pluck at the wrapper.

"Megan, you know that I would have gotten you on birth control if you had told me that you were going to start having sex," Sheila said with a stern but loving tone.

"It's not like it works anyway," she muttered.

"What's that supposed to mean?" Sheila narrowed her eyes again, but this time there wasn't a hint of humor. "Because *I* got pregnant?"

"No," Megan sighed heavily, pushing the paper away from her. She looked up at Sheila and shook her head. "I tried taking them. They didn't work."

I leaned back in my seat and eyed Brooke cautiously, wondering if we should step aside and give them some privacy to discuss this. Instead, she leaned forward and rested her elbows on the table as she waited for them to go on.

"Where did you get birth control?" Sheila asked, her voice rising a full octave.

"I borrowed some."

"You *borrowed* someone's birth control?" Sheila shook her head and rubbed her temples with her fingers. "Megan, you can't just borrow peoples' medicine that you don't know. That's not how it works, and it could be really dangerous."

"It wasn't just *anyone,* mom. I'm not *that* stupid." She huffed and folded her arms over her chest.

"Okay, then whose did you take?"

"Yours."

Brooke and I let out a small gasp at the same time. I covered my mouth and felt my jaw drop as I stared at Sheila, waiting for the smoke to start puffing out of the top of her head.

"Megan Renee Roberts!" Sheila's voice boomed through the small bakery. Thankfully, no one else was in here, but Ryder came rushing out to see what the fuss was all about. Brooke lifted her hand and waved him back into the kitchen as we sat and watched the rest of the drama unfold. I was surprised that Parker hadn't heard the commotion from his office in the back, but maybe it was better that he wasn't there for this.

"You took my birth control?"

"Not the full pack," she said defensively.

"How many did you take?"

"I don't know. A few?"

"What the hell were you thinking?"

"I was trying *not* to get pregnant. Duh."

I bit down on my bottom lip, fighting the urge to say something. Sheila closed her eyes and leaned back against the chair. I wanted to be helpful without overstepping, but by the looks of it, Sheila needed all of the help she could get right now.

"That's um, not really how birth control works," I said lightly, pulling Megan's attention to me. "You have to take the pills daily for them to prevent pregnancy. If you miss one—or a few—it can make them ineffective that month, meaning that you would need to use another form of birth control."

She stared blankly at me as if I had just told her some ridiculous math riddle that I needed her to solve.

"By taking your mom's pills, it made her birth control ineffective that month, which is how she got pregnant."

Her eyes widened with shock as she turned to look at Sheila.

"It's *my* fault that you got pregnant?" she whispered, covering her mouth.

"Yes and no," she shrugged. "Yes, because you took my birth control which screwed up the month, but no because I should have been paying attention to notice that some were missing. But honestly, Megan, how did you not know how they worked? Why didn't you come ask me?"

I felt the tug in my heart as I thought back to the awkward conversation that I had with my mom after I had sex for the first time. I can't say that I knew much more than Megan did, but I was also younger and didn't feel like I could ask the questions that I needed the answers to before I made such a life-changing decision.

"I was afraid that you would be mad at me," she admitted.

"For asking about birth control?"

"For wanting to have sex."

The front door chimed as it opened. Brooke got up and walked behind the counter to greet the customer.

"Honey, you're sixteen years old. I'm not surprised that this is something that you would start thinking about. Honestly, I wish that you would have waited, or at least come talk to me first, but I'm not mad at you."

"I love you, mama," Megan said, leaning over to hug her.

"I love you too. Now go check in with Ryder and see if he needs any help around here. If you're gonna have a baby, you're gonna start learning how to take care of yourself, and that means getting a job."

"Mama," Megan whined with a frown.

"Now." She pointed to the kitchen and waited while Megan got up and left to find Ryder.

After a few minutes, she let out a heavy sigh and closed her eyes.

"What in the world am I going to do with *two* babies at the same time?" she asked, looking at me with a desperation in her eyes that I had only seen once before when Parker was missing.

"It'll be alright," I assured her even though I had no idea whether it would be or not. "You guys will figure it out. You always do."

"She's still just a baby herself, and here she is, having one. I know that I'm going to have to help her raise it, and I just don't know that I have it in me to even start over again with my own. That makes me a terrible person, doesn't it?"

I thought about my answer for a moment before I responded.

"No," I shook my head. "It doesn't make you a terrible person. It makes you an honest one who is genuinely concerned for these babies and making sure that they have the best lives possible. *That* makes you a wonderful person."

She smiled softly and pulled her shoulders back as she inhaled slowly. The customer left, and Brooke went to the back with Megan and Ryder as Parker headed up front.

"Hey," he said happily, walking over to where we were sitting. He leaned down and kissed Sheila. "I heard Megan talking to Ryder. I didn't know you guys were here. How'd your appointments go?"

He pulled out the barstool beside her and cupped his hands over hers. I got up to leave and give them some privacy but her eyes immediately locked onto mine.

"You can stay Gen, we don't need privacy," she assured me.

"The appointments went well," Sheila said, giving Parker her full attention. "Megan and I are both due on July 10th."

"You're both due on the same day?" he asked in disbelief, as a crooked smile spread across his face. "What's the chances of that happening?"

Sheila and I looked at each other and burst into laughter.

"Pretty good, actually," she said with a chuckle. "It turns out that Megan thought that she only needed to take a birth control pill when she had sex, so she was *borrowing* mine. I hadn't noticed that any were missing, therefore, I got pregnant, and she didn't know that she needed the entire months' worth, so she got pregnant too."

Parker's eyes widened as his hands fell from Sheila's and landed on the table with a thud.

"Woah."

"Yeah," she agreed lightly. "So, there you have it. We're both pregnant and due at the same time because she decided that we should share a pack of birth control."

"That's so crazy. But everything is alright with the baby? Both babies?"

She let out a laugh, patting his hand gently.

"Yes, my love. Both babies are perfectly fine and growing how they should be right now. We're both around eight weeks, and we'll go back for another ultrasound in four weeks."

"Okay, I'll make sure that I can be there for that one. I'm sorry that I couldn't make it this morning."

I sat there watching them, happy that my dad had finally found someone he loved so wholeheartedly.

"Thank you for going with them this morning, Gen. That really meant a lot to me," he said, turning to me.

"No problem, I enjoyed being there. It was an honor to see the babies and hear their heartbeats."

"You got to hear the heartbeat?" Parker asked excitedly, turning to Sheila.

She nodded happily as I reached into my pocket and pulled out my phone.

"I hope you don't mind, but I recorded it for you," I said, sliding my phone over to them. "Just push the play button."

Parker did as instructed and covered his mouth as his eyes teared up when he saw the ultrasound image on the screen and heard the baby's heartbeat. I hadn't *intended* to get a good shot of the cute doctor as well but found myself grinning when I saw his side profile in the corner of the video.

"I'll send it to you guys so you have a copy,' I offered as he passed my phone back to me.

"I can't believe that we're having a baby," he whispered, looking down at her stomach. "This is so *unreal*."

"I'm really happy for you guys," I said, feeling myself get choked up. It was true, I was happy for them. It was a fresh start with a new life, and I found myself a little jealous of it. Not that I wanted to have a baby right now, but just the excitement that was in the air around us from the new life that was coming.

"Hey, Gen, I wanted to talk to you," Parker said, clearing his throat. He shifted awkwardly, and I could tell that he was uncomfortable with whatever he was about to say. "I know that I wasn't there for you much when you were growing up, and I'm really sorry about that. I wish that I could go back and change things, but I can't. But I hope that you know that I would go to the ends of the earth to make you happy and that I'm so glad you're back in my life. I know that it doesn't change your childhood, and I'm sorry about that."

He was starting to ramble, and suddenly, I got what he was trying to say.

"Dad," I said calmly, loving the look on his face when I called him that instead of Parker. "I'm okay, you don't have to apologize for my childhood. I had a great one, and I understand why things happened the way that they did. You do *not* need to feel guilty about having another child and being there from the beginning with this one, so please don't."

His face was etched with worry, and I felt bad that he was so torn up about this.

"Really—I promise. I'm fine, and I'm super excited to be a big sister again. It'll be fun having new babies in the family."

"Does that mean that you're going to stick around for a while?" Sheila asked with a smile. I could see the hope on both of their faces as they waited for me to say yes.

The answer was right there on the tip of my tongue, but yet I couldn't get it out.

"I'm not sure how long I'll be in town," I said, feeling the knot in my stomach.

Six

Tanner

"Are there any more patients on the schedule for today?" I called up to Dottie at the front desk as I finished my notes in the file I had been working on.

"No, Doctor Hayes, your schedule is free for the rest of the day."

"Please, call me Tanner," I said, as I walked up to her desk and set the file down.

I looked around at the empty waiting room, surprised that no one else was waiting.

"So that's it? No one else?"

"Nope, not until…." She pushed her glasses up her face and leaned closer to the computer screen. "Tomorrow at eleven am. Ms. Dodson will be in for her annual exam."

"Wow, okay then." I shrugged, unsure of what to do with my downtime.

"How was your first day?" she asked, leaning away from the computer and turning to face me.

"It was fine, a lot slower than I had expected," I admitted, leaning against the wall behind me. "I'm used to seeing more than three patients in a day. Doctor Long didn't give me too many details on what to expect when I took the job," I laughed, wondering if she was worried that I would change my mind when I heard how slow it would be.

"She usually only sees three or four a day when she's here, though it's split up more to fill out the whole day. You got a doozy with yours all lined up, back to back." She laughed and shook her head as if we had been through some major rush.

"Well, the first one was a two for one special," I joked, remembering the three women who waited for me in the exam room this morning. I hadn't known what to expect, but I was a little blindsided by the trio—but in a good way.

I had taken the time when I was writing my notes down to look through the files and found that the two I had seen were related, mother and daughter. It made sense given that they looked alike with their pale skin and light blue eyes—and the fiery red hair. But the other girl that was with them was the complete opposite. She had long, dark hair that offset the emerald green eyes that widened the moment she saw me. The fair skin that blushed the perfect shade of red as she tried to avoid my heated gaze. I had seen plenty of beautiful women before, but there was something about her that immediately grabbed my attention and made me want to keep it there.

"It's such a shame," Dottie said, interrupting my thoughts as I imagined her plump pink lips against my mouth.

"What is?" I asked, furrowing my brow in confusion.

"That little Megan Roberts is *pregnant,*" she whispered as if anyone was around to hear us. "Her mama is a good woman, but Lord knows, she's had her hands full with four kids. After her husband up and left her, she had to raise them all on her own. No wonder her daughter is in the same position she was."

"Well, I don't know how Doctor Long likes to do things here, however, where I come from, it's in poor taste to gossip about the patients we see or discuss the reason for their visit. Please let me know if you'd like for me to pull up a copy of the privacy disclosure that I recently signed with my new hire paperwork, I'd be happy to loan it to you as a refresher."

She snapped her mouth shut and glared at me. I knew this wasn't the best way to make friends in a new—and incredibly *small* town, but I was never one to gossip about people. I sure as hell wasn't about to start now.

Seven

Gen

"Ugh, are they making *you* work here too?" Megan groaned as she came out from the kitchen of The Sweet Shop. I was leaning against the counter behind the register, waiting for Brooke to get back. She had asked if I could help out for a few minutes while she ran to the store to grab some more sugar after scolding Ryder for forgetting to put it on their order this week.

"No, I'm just helping out for a few minutes while Brooke is gone," I said.

"Well, be thankful that they're not making you work here. It's such a drag and *soo* boring."

"I'm sure there are worse jobs out there," I laughed, thinking back to the summer that I worked as a mascot for the baseball team. Wearing a giant, furry bumblebee costume was hard enough, but add in the heat and humidity, and it was downright miserable.

"I don't know why I have to have one. My mom thinks that she can just boss me around and force me to do whatever she says, but I'm gonna be a mom soon, and all of that is going to stop."

I scrunched my face and shook my head. If only she knew just how hard it was without your mom, then maybe she wouldn't be complaining about hers.

"She means well," I said lightly, not wanting to get into an argument this early in the day.

"I just know that she's going to try to tell me what to do and how to do things. She never waits to see if I can figure it out on my own. Instead, she just pushes until she gets her way. You're so lucky that you don't have to go through that," she scoffed.

I sucked in a breath and forced myself to hold it to keep from saying something that I shouldn't.

Her face reddened when she realized what she had said.

"Oh my God, Gen! I'm so sorry. I didn't mean—"

"It's okay," I said quickly, putting my hand up to stop her. "But I see a car outside, so I'd get back to work before Brooke comes in."

I didn't know if it was her car for sure, but I was desperate to shift the conversation to *anything* other than my mom.

Megan nodded and grabbed the basket of cleaning supplies she had brought out with her, and started wiping down the tables. I let out the breath that I had been holding and tried to get my nerves to calm down again. The bell chimed as the door opened, the bright morning sun reflecting off of the glass and almost blinding me. I held up my hand to shield my eyes, assuming that it was Brooke.

"Did you bring me something sweet?" I teased, trying to make a joke out of the bags of sugar I knew she was bringing back. I lowered my hand and felt my heart skip a beat when I saw that it wasn't Brooke after all. Instead, it was the hot doctor from the clinic.

The sun filtered into the room, casting a warm glow on his short, blonde hair that looked effortlessly tousled on his head. He walked across the room with the confidence of someone who knew that every woman would stop in their tracks for a good look at him. As he got closer, I felt my stomach tighten, unsure of what to say.

"I thought *you* were supposed to have something sweet for *me*," he teased, pointing to the sign above me that read: The Sweet Shop.

"Oh, um," I laughed nervously, twirling a strand of hair around my finger as his charcoal grey eyes watched me. "Sure. We have everything. What can I get you?"

He took the last few steps to the counter and kept his eyes on me for a few seconds before lowering to look inside the pastry case that Brooke had stocked this morning before she left. I took the opportunity to check him out, noticing how fit his body looked in the snug t-shirt and jeans compared to the scrubs he was wearing the other day at the clinic.

"Everything looks delicious," he said softly, continuing to admire the selection. "What do you recommend?"

I felt the heat from his gaze as it traveled over my body as he stood up and locked eyes on me.

"I don't know," I stammered. "What do you like?"

"I like everything."

"Well… then… um…," I panicked for a moment, trying to figure out what to say. It was like he was sucking all of the brain power out of me with some weird Jedi mind tricks.

"What's your favorite?" he asked, the corners of his lips turning up into a smile as he took a few steps to the side, and I moved behind the case.

"My favorite?" I repeated, my voice suddenly squeaky.

"Mmhmm."

"I guess it would be the cream cheese danish especially if it's warmed up. The cream in the middle gets nice and warm—it's like an explosion on your tongue."

I felt the heat prickle my skin as the blush quickly spread over me, completely mortified by the words I had just spoken. *What the hell? An explosion on your tongue?*

I tried to shake it off and pretend that it hadn't happened, but when he pulled his lower lip in between his teeth to keep from laughing, I knew that he had read into it the same way that I had.

Before I could say anything more, I heard the bell chime as the door opened. I prayed that it was Brooke, because I definitely couldn't be trusted to watch her store while she was gone. I heard their laughter as she and Sheila headed our way.

"How's it going?" Brooke asked, looking between us with a curious smile on her face. She set the bags of sugar down on the counter and stood next to me. I glanced over at Sheila, as she set her bags down with the others. She was oblivious to the fact that her doctor was standing in front of me and responsible for the crimson blush on my face.

"I was just telling—I don't think I got your name," he paused, staring deep into my eyes as he pinned me in place.

"Gen," I whispered.

"Right—Gen, that I was looking for something sweet to satisfy this new craving that I have, and she kindly recommended the cream cheese danish." He continued to hold my gaze as he spoke to Brooke.

"Well, let me get those packed up for you," Brooke said with a touch of uncertainty in her voice. "How many would you like?"

"Two, please. And warmed up, if you don't mind."

"Sure, I'll have these ready for you in a few minutes."

Brooke quietly worked beside me, reaching in to grab the pastries while I tried to look anywhere but at him.

"What's the name for the order?" Brooke asked casually, pulling out a pen to write on the pastry bag.

He looked around the shop, noticing that there were no other customers. I knew what she was doing and tried to hide the nervous laughter that was threatening to boil over inside of me. This was all too much, and I was a flustered mess.

"Rushes come in out of nowhere," Brooke lied with a smile. "I would hate to give someone else your perfectly warmed-up cream cheese danishes that Gen was so kind to recommend."

I watched the dimples in his cheeks deepen as he grinned and looked over at Brooke.

"Tanner."

She smiled and jotted the name down before heading to the kitchen, linking arms with Sheila as she dragged her in with her.

"So, how long have you worked here?" he asked, sitting on the edge of the table behind him.

"I don't, I was just helping out while she ran to the store."

"I see," he chuckled.

"What's that supposed to mean?" I asked a tad defensively. I was already feeling self-conscious and overly exposed from being this close to him. It was like he could read every single insecurity that I had.

"Nothing," he laughed harder and held his hands up in front of him. "I just didn't expect your level of expertise with the pastries this morning. That's all."

"Hey—you asked what I liked, and I told you," I teased, his laughter calming me. He wasn't a scary man, just so incredibly good-looking that I felt myself freezing around him and tripping over my own words.

"Well, it's nice to see a woman who knows what she likes."

The look on his face didn't go unnoticed by me, but before I could come up with a witty comeback, Brooke and Sheila came out with his order.

"Here you go, Tanner," Brooke said, handing him the bag with his name on it.

"Thank you, how much do I owe you?"

"It's on the house," she replied easily, coming to stand behind the counter with me.

"Thank you for the generous offer, but please, I insist on paying."

"Well, technically, Gen was helping you, so you guys can work out the payment details together."

I could hear the not-so-hidden innuendos laced in her words and tried to scowl at her as she looked away.

"Hey, Sheila, can you help me put these away?" Brooke said awkwardly, pointing to the bags of sugar and nodding her head so hard that I was afraid she was going to need a chiropractor to adjust it back to its normal position.

Once they were gone, he leaned closer to the counter and locked eyes with me. I felt the heat prickle my skin again as my body temperature rose a degree or two.

"I would love to take you to dinner sometime," he offered with a smile that felt like it would melt my panties off right then and there. "You know, for payment," he added, raising his bag in the air and sending the heavenly aroma through the space between us. Without thinking about it, I closed my eyes and took in a deep breath, my mouth salivating when I remembered how delicious they tasted.

When I opened them, I found him staring intently at me, his Adam's apple bobbing as he swallowed hard.

"You don't have to take me to dinner, really," I said quickly, suddenly nervous with the way he was looking at me. My heart started racing, making my palms sweaty. I pulled the sleeves of my sweater down a tad to try to dry my hands.

"Nothing would give me more pleasure," he insisted, his voice flirtier than before.

"I'm not sure when I would be free," I lied. "I'm supposed to head home soon."

"Where's home?"

"Arkansas."

A flash of disappointment crossed his face before he subtly

shook it away and smiled again.

"Well then, how about tonight?"

"I, um…" I was struggling to come up with an excuse, when I heard Sheila pipe up from the kitchen.

"She's free tonight," she hollered loudly before giggling with Brooke.

I felt my body stiffen in response. There was no way that I could go to dinner with him. I would make a complete fool of myself. I had already done so a handful of times in the short amount of time he had been there this morning.

"Perfect," he said with a shit-eating grin. "Here's my card. My cell is at the bottom. And since I'm worried you're gonna pull a Cinderella move on me later, why don't I pick you up here?"

I heard more giggling and turned to glare at the door. I sighed heavily, folding my arms over my chest, as I turned back to him.

"I don't know," I countered again. "I don't even know you."

"Well, I have heard that most people do that over dinner— you know, get to know the other person while sharing a meal?"

I pulled my lips together and rubbed them back and forth. Why was I so nervous about this? It's not like he was asking me to go to some seedy dark alley with him in the middle of the night. It was just dinner in Stone Creek. Everyone here would be talking about it anyway, so I was probably safer than I'd ever been on a date before. Once word got out that I was going on a date, I could bet that Parker would find a reason to be in the area, just in case I needed him. He was funny like that.

"Alright," I said softly, my resolve starting to wear off.

"Great," he rushed out, probably afraid that I would change my mind if given a chance. "I'll be here at seven."

"Okay," I mumbled, feeling a mix of butterflies and nausea at the same time.

"Have a nice day, ladies," he called out by the kitchen door where they were hiding, waving two fingers in the air as he left. "I'll see you tonight, Gen." He looked over his shoulder and shot me another panty-dropping smile.

The door opened, and a gust of cold air whipped in, slapping me in the face. What in the world had I just gotten myself into?

Eight

Gen

"What did you guys just do?" I hissed, pushing through the kitchen doors and swatting at Brooke and Sheila who were crouched on the floor, giggling.

"What?! He was cute and *totally* into you," Brooke squealed.

"He is *not* into me," I objected. "I just made a complete ass out of myself in front of him, and now, he probably thinks that I'm some bimbo who will be an easy lay."

"Why on earth would he think that? What happened before we got here?" Sheila asked, pulling back the liner on the cupcake that Brooke had given her.

"Nothing," I sighed. "He was asking for recommendations, and I got overly detailed about the danishes and may or may not have said something along the lines of how the warm cream explodes on your tongue."

Their eyes bulged out as they covered their mouths with their hands, trying to hide their laughter.

"I know, I know," I whined. "It's terrible! I didn't realize that I had said it until it was too late."

I looked down at my boot and rubbed the toe of it along the black mark on the tile.

"It's pretty funny," Sheila admitted, taking a bite out of her dessert. "I don't think it was that bad."

"Oh, I'm sure he's just waiting to take me out tonight so he can *show me* how cream explodes on your tongue," I said dryly.

"I don't know if it's just because I'm pregnant, but that sounded way dirtier than it should have been."

"That's because I meant it to be dirty," I laughed. "Because *he's* going to think of it in a dirty way. He's probably sitting in his office, eating his damn pastries, and envisioning some gross picture from some overrated porn site."

"I think you're being overly dramatic," Brooke said, coming to stand beside me. She patted my back and then handed me a cupcake. "I know that it's not a cream cheese danish, but trust me—the double fudge frosting is even better. I don't need the dirty details of it—just eat it and save those for your date," she teased.

"It's not a date," I objected. "It's just dinner so he can pay what he owes for the damn pastries. Which I have to admit—you guys have a weird way of doing business down here." I shook my head and licked the frosting, pulling a dollop onto my tongue and letting the rich flavors sit there for a few seconds before I swallowed.

"It *IS* a date and a cute one at that. He seems totally into you, Gen. Why don't you want to go?" Sheila asked softly.

"I just don't want to give him the wrong idea—which I already have. Besides, he's gorgeous—he can literally get any woman he wants—why would he want to go on a date with me?"

I took another bite, letting my worries go with the sugar-induced high that I was on.

"I don't know him," Sheila said around a mouthful of cake. "But he seems nice. Besides, it's just one date. You don't have to see him again after that, if you don't want to."

I pushed the last bite into my mouth and thought about what she said.

"What do you mean you don't know him?" I asked, swallowing hard to force the thickness of the frosting down.

"He's new in town, nobody knows him," Brooke answered. "But from what I've been hearing, Doctor Long said that they're suddenly seeing a boost in patients with everyone wanting to come in for annual checkups. Apparently, the women here are willing to drop their panties for Doctor Hayes."

She wiggled her eyebrows suggestively, and I rolled my eyes, knowing that I was easily one of those women. Hell,

I was ready to take them off and throw them at him just from the look he gave me while we talked about orgasmic pastries.

"Does it bother you that I would be going on a date with your doctor?" I asked Sheila.

"Why would it?"

"Well, because… you know. He'll have seen you down there already, and then if we…." I let my thoughts trail off, unable to force them out of my throat.

"You mean you're worried that if *you* have sex with Tanner, it might be weird for Sheila because he's also seen her vagina, and she's dating your dad?" Brooke offered, looking between us.

"Well… Yeah." My cheeks burned from the flush of heat spreading over them, as I talked to them about this.

"Trust me, Gen, it doesn't bother me at all. What he does is completely professional—for both of us. But, if it makes you uncomfortable, I can ask Doctor Long to take over once she's back. I don't have to go back for a few weeks anyway."

I pushed myself up onto the counter against the wall and thought about it. I didn't want to make her switch doctors, especially if she really wanted to see Tanner. But at the same time, I couldn't help but wonder if it would be weird that he had seen her down there. I had to keep reminding myself that it was just one date, and I would be leaving soon, so it shouldn't matter either way.

<u>Nine</u>

Tanner

"Who's next on the schedule?" I asked Dottie from across the office. Today was supposed to be slow, that's why I took my time to stop for breakfast before I came in. It was just an added bonus that I ran into Gen at The Sweet Shop. I couldn't get her out of my mind after I left and found myself thinking about how flustered she was. I pictured her flushed cheeks while eating the danishes in my office this morning—behind a closed door. I felt like I was fifteen again, getting an erection at just the thought of something sexual with a beautiful girl.

"You have Joleen Palmer at one o'clock, Doris Jaden at one fifteen, Loretta Jones at one-thirty, and then Janie Lewis at two o'clock."

I glanced at my watch. It was already 12:55, which meant that I had five minutes before the next patient.

"I thought you said that today was a light day?" I asked with a hint of annoyance.

"It was. Most of these were scheduled this morning."

I ran a hand down the scruff on my face and sighed. I was going to regret asking this.

"Do I even want to know why?"

"You can't go jogging at the park, shirtless, and not get the women around here talking," she laughed, walking into my office with the stack of files for the patients that I needed to see.

"Apparently not," I mumbled under my breath.

"Ms. Palmer is in room one, she's already changed into her gown. Ms. Jaden is also checked into her room. I'll work on getting the other two situated once you're ready."

I looked down at the files and fought the chuckle, when I noticed what they were all here for today: annual checkups and pap smears.

Today was going to be a long day, but at least I had a date with a beautiful girl to look forward to.

After a long day of convincing women that I did not need to be between their legs longer than necessary, I was having a hard time clearing my head. I was thankful to have a nurse with me in the rooms for each exam, but that didn't stop the women from making side comments and asking if I was single. Small town life was completely different than the big city, and I was starting to wonder what I had gotten myself into.

By four o'clock, I was done and leaving the office to get ready. I had plenty of time to kill, so I stopped by the store and stocked up on groceries and a few bottles of wine—just in case I needed them this weekend. We didn't get much snow in Los Angeles, so I didn't know what to expect when the news reported a heavy winter storm this weekend. Better safe than sorry was my motto.

I took a shower and got ready, anxious to go pick Gen up at seven. I wasn't sure if the shop even stayed open that late, but I didn't want to give her the chance to say no. Maybe it was overly selfish of me, but there was something about her that pulled me in and made me want to spend more time with her—even if it was limited.

I hated the idea of her leaving and had no idea how long she would be in Stone Creek before she had to go back to Arkansas. I was hoping to find out more information tonight, if I could get it out of her. She was young and beautiful—I just didn't know *how* young she was.

By 6:45, I was heading over to The Sweet Shop. My nerves were a wild mess of excitement along with some first date jitters. I pulled into a parking spot by the front door and got out, not stopping to take one last quick look in the mirror. While I wanted to make sure I looked okay, I didn't want anyone to see that I doubted myself. If I knew one thing about women—it was how much they loved a confident man, and that's what I was aiming for tonight.

I opened the door and walked inside. I was surprised that they were still open and had a handful of customers scattered around the room at the different tables. The other woman that was there this morning looked up from behind the register and smiled, giving me a quick wave.

I headed that way when I didn't see Gen.

"She's in the back, she'll be out soon."

I smiled and felt the rush of panic disappear as quickly as it came on.

"I'm Brooke, by the way," she said, extending her hand over the counter to me. "I didn't realize that I hadn't introduced myself this morning until after you left. Sorry about that."

"No worries," I assured her, letting go of her hand when I heard the kitchen door open. I turned to look and felt my heart skip a beat when I saw Gen standing there, looking more amazing than ever.

Her long dark hair was pulled up, exposing her slender neck that begged to be kissed. Red lipstick brought my attention to her lips as she nervously licked them, instantly making my dick hard. I looked up to find her green eyes studying me, the smoky makeup intensifying the sexiness that was radiating off of her.

I swallowed hard, trying to find the words to say as she walked over to me. Her slender figure was on full display in the tight jeans she was wearing with knee-high black boots that had a super thin heel that made them even sexier. The cream-colored sweater was the only thing that pulled the outfit in some and didn't scream *sex* to me, even though it was wrapped snuggly around her full breasts.

"You look amazing," I whispered, letting my eyes leisurely travel the length of her body again. She shyly tucked her chin and looked away.

"Thank you," she said quietly.

"Are you ready to go?"

I was suddenly eager to get out of here and be alone with her. Maybe it was because I was excited to spend time with her, or maybe it was just because I didn't need the folks of Stone Creek talking about the new doctor with the boner in the middle of the bakery on a Friday night.

She nodded and smiled, though I could see her nerves were just as bad as mine right now. I hoped that it was more excitement than anything else, but I wasn't sure.

"It was nice seeing you again," I said to Brooke before walking away.

"You too," she smiled and looked at Gen like a mother would. "Where are you guys going tonight?"

I cleared my throat, suddenly feeling a little nervous like I would if I were meeting her parents for the first time.

"I made a reservation at Genaro's."

"In Clarksville?" Brooke asked, her eyebrows shooting up in disbelief.

"Yeah... why?" I eyed her suspiciously.

"I hate to break it to you, but I don't think you're going to make it. The storm has already started moving in, and I heard that they might shut down the highway out there soon because of decreased visibility."

Son of a bitch!

"I hadn't heard," I groaned through clenched teeth. I had spent the morning looking up the nicest restaurants around Stone Creek and finally decided that it might be a good idea to go somewhere in another town to keep the gossip mill to a minimum.

"You might be able to find something in town, but a lot of places will be closing early tonight. The storm is supposed to be a bad one."

I looked at Gen with despair in my eyes, hating that my plans had already fallen through.

"I'm sorry, Gen. I had no idea. We don't get much snow where I'm from, so I didn't know what to expect with this storm they've been talking about."

"It's okay," she said quickly, and I knew that she was taking this opportunity to cancel the date. "We can go somewhere else if you want?"

I pulled my head back in surprise. She wasn't canceling?

"I don't know where to go," I replied slowly, trying to think as I spoke. "The only place I can offer is my house, but I don't want you to think that I'm—"

"It's fine," she assured me, resting her hand on my arm. "If you want to stop and grab some groceries, I can cook something for us. Or we can always grab a pizza and take it back to your place?"

"Actually, I just picked up groceries this morning, so I can cook for you if you'd like?"

"That sounds amazing."

I smiled and felt on top of the world as we said goodbye to Brooke and got into my car. It was a quick drive to my place, but the anticipation of spending time with Gen without any interruptions made it feel like it was taking forever.

Ten

Gen

"That smells amazing," I said, as I leaned over the island and watched him stir the sauce he was making.

"Thank you, it's one of my favorites. It's a creamy garlic penne dish that I like to make when I'm craving something savory."

I didn't comment on the *creamy* part but felt my mouth watering at the thought. I watched as he moved around the kitchen effortlessly with his sleeves rolled up, showing off the definition in his arms. I felt a tingle between my thighs as I watched his hands, noticing the gentle way he worked the knife as he cut the cooked chicken breasts into thin slices before tossing them in the pan with the sauce and noodles.

I was practically drooling into my wine glass, and it didn't have anything to do with the heavenly aroma floating around me. I took another sip and looked up to find his eyes on me, watching my mouth as my lips parted to take a drink.

My breathing grew heavy as he licked his lips and let his eyes roam down my body. I swallowed the sip of wine and felt the tingles shooting through every nerve in my body.

He reached over and grabbed the bottle of pinot noir and raised his eyebrows to ask before refilling my glass. I nodded and extended it toward him, feeling the electricity between us as his fingers grazed mine in the process. I pulled my glass back and took another sip, fighting the urge to jump over the counter and kiss him.

I didn't know what had gotten into me. Maybe it was the idea that I could have whatever fun I wanted to now because I would be leaving soon, so there was no risk of commitment or having to deal with any awkwardness later. Or perhaps it was the glass of wine that I had with Brooke while she and Sheila helped me get ready for the date and talked me into living in the moment, enjoying whatever tonight turned out to be.

He refilled his glass and took a quick sip, his lips glistening before he licked them and set the glass down.

"Alright, dinner is ready," he said, walking over to the stove and turning off the burner. He filled both plates and carried them over to the table before pulling my seat out for me.

I smiled and sat down, setting my wine in front of me while I waited for him to join me. A few minutes later, he came over and set a basket of bread on the table between us and sat down.

My stomach growled, and I felt the need to put something in my body other than wine. Not that food was exactly what

I wanted inside of me at the moment, but it was a good start to soak up some of the alcohol that was swimming around, making my insides feel slushy.

"This looks and smells amazing, thank you," I said as I pierced a noodle with my fork and took a bite. The flavor was so intense that I closed my eyes and let out a soft moan as I chewed. "Oh my God," I moaned quietly.

I heard a low chuckle, and my eyes fluttered open to look at him. He was leaning back in his chair with his arms folded loosely over his chest as he watched me.

"Sorry," I muttered, embarrassed as I tried to look away.

"For what?" he said seductively. "It's hot as hell when you make that sound—don't ever apologize for it."

I rubbed my lips together nervously, unsure of what to say. We stayed there, staring at each other for a few minutes before he spoke again.

"I guess you have a thing for warm, creamy things?" He arched a brow as his dimples deepened with his grin.

I hid my face in my hands and laughed. It was so embarrassing, but when he joined in, it lightened the mood.

"I still can't believe I said that," I admitted, peeking at him through my fingers. "But, yeah, I guess we can say that it's true." I looked down at the plate of delicious food in front of me, remembering the taste that teased my tongue a few minutes ago and sent me into this state of bliss that I didn't want to come out of.

"You know what you like, there's nothing shameful about that," he said, his voice still lower than before.

"What do you like?" I asked, suddenly feeling bold. I took another bite, making sure I didn't moan loudly with this one.

"I feel like that's a loaded question," he said, his charcoal eyes darkening.

"Fair enough," I laughed after finishing my bite. "Okay, what do you like to eat?"

There was so much sexual tension in the air that I could practically hear it sizzle and crackle between us.

"There aren't many things that I won't eat. I have a pretty diverse palate."

I nodded and took another bite. I noticed how tight his jaw was as he took a bite and chewed, his eyes fully focused on every move I made.

"What brought you to Stone Creek?" I asked, trying to fill the silence and get out from his penetrating stare. If he didn't stop, we would both be naked and going at it on his living room floor in a matter of minutes. I could see it in his eyes—he was feeling the same thing that I was.

"Work," he said before taking another bite.

I could tell that he didn't want to say more than that, so I let it be. We ate in silence for a few minutes before he turned the questions back around on me.

"What about you?" he asked.

"My dad lives here. I came to visit for the holiday."

"The rest of your family is in Arkansas?"

I bit my lip, trying to keep it from trembling.

"They used to be."

He lowered his fork to the plate and folded his hands in front of him, giving me his full attention.

"Used to be?"

I swallowed hard, trying to force the emotions down that were threatening to bubble up.

"My mom passed away a few months ago. My step-dad and siblings are moving to Alabama in a few weeks to be closer to his family."

He gave me a sad smile as I lifted my glass and took a sip.

"I'm very sorry for your loss."

"Thank you," I whispered, pushing my noodles around the plate with my fork.

"If you don't mind me asking, what's in Arkansas?"

I set my fork down and sighed heavily before looking up at him.

"Honestly? I don't know. Nothing, I guess." I shrugged and shook my head as I looked away to keep him from seeing the tears that were dotting the corners of my eyes. "I haven't figured out where I'm supposed to be, so I just assumed that I would go back there. It's where I grew up, but I don't have anyone left there."

"Why don't you stay in Stone Creek? You said your dad is here, right?"

There was an odd pleading tone in how he said it, almost as if *he* wanted me to stay.

"I don't know," I answered honestly. "He has his hands full already, and now he has a baby on the way. I don't want to get in the way."

"I doubt anyone could ever think that about you."

I felt the corners of my lips tug upward into a smile.

We talked through the rest of dinner, sticking to lighter topics like the weather in LA and how funny small-town people are when someone new shows up. It was nice to feel so connected to him on so many different levels. By the time we were done, I got up to take my dishes to the sink when he stopped me.

"I'll take it," he said, his hand lightly touching mine before I could pick up the plate. We stood inches apart, and the heat radiated between us.

"I can help, I don't mind," I said quietly, looking up into the liquid pools of desire.

"It's okay. Why don't you go make yourself comfortable on the couch, and I'll be there in a minute?"

I nodded and pulled my hand back, my heart racing in my chest and a slow ache starting to build between my legs.

I waited for him to grab the plate and head to the kitchen before I sucked in a clean breath of air that wasn't laced with his intoxicating scent and went to the living room. The snow was falling outside, covering everything in a beautiful blanket of white. I was leaning against the wall, watching the peacefulness of the snow, when I heard his soft footsteps behind me.

"I should walk away and give you space," he whispered in my ear as his hands rested lightly on my hips. "But you're like a drug that I can't stay away from. You're so addicting that I find myself wanting more the closer I get to you. So if you want me to, I can take you home before anything happens. Because I can't promise you that I'll be able to keep my distance from you if you stay."

I could feel his heart beating wildly in his chest as it pressed against my back, the hard bulge in his jeans a clear indicator of how bad he wanted this as it rubbed against my ass when he moved.

"Do you want me to take you home, Gen?"

I closed my eyes and sucked in a long, slow breath. My mom's last words to me constantly played over and over in my head—*don't be afraid to live life and be happy.*

I turned to look at him, our bodies pushed against each other.

"No," I whispered.

He pinched his eyes shut as I ran my hands up his chest, feeling the hard, rigid muscles underneath.

"Gen," he hissed in warning. "If you do that, I might not be able to stop myself."

"I don't want you to stop," I said eagerly. "I don't want either of us to stop tonight. I just want to live in the moment, Tanner."

"Are you sure?" he asked through clenched teeth. "I need you to be real clear on what you want, Gen. Tell me."

I looked into his hooded eyes and wrapped my arms around his neck.

"I want you to fuck me until I can't see straight."

I heard a low growl from his throat before he reached down and picked me up, tossing me over his shoulder as he carried me to bed.

Eleven

Tanner

The first thing that I was going to do after tonight was buy Gen a new pair of shoes that came off in one quick pull. I loved how sexy her boots were—and I was tempted to fuck her with them on, but given that I desperately wanted to see her completely naked, I had to take the time to get them off.

She giggled as I tugged and pulled and struggled to free her of the fashionable death contraptions before she reached down and unzipped them. Apparently, any brain cells that I had were functioning in the *wrong* head since I hadn't noticed that easy trick. Within seconds, her boots were off, and I was pulling her jeans down her long legs and throwing them to the floor.

I couldn't keep my eyes off of her as she laid on my bed, her eyes filled with desire that radiated out of her. I wanted to savor every inch of her and take my time making love to her, but at this rate, I was going to be lucky to last three seconds. She was so fucking gorgeous that I could barely keep it together long enough to get us undressed.

Once her clothes were off, I pulled my shirt over my head and tossed it to the floor. Her eyes widened as she licked her lips as she checked me out. I quickly stepped out of my jeans and hooked my thumbs into the waistband of my boxer briefs before sliding them down and letting my erection spring free. Her jaw dropped open, and I couldn't wait to see my cock inside of that beautiful mouth of hers.

I walked over to the bed and climbed on top of her, propping myself up on my elbow as I gently stroked her cheek before kissing her. The kiss started soft but quickly got more heated as our bodies eagerly waited to explore each other. I trailed kisses down her neck and along her collarbone before working my way down her chest. My tongue ran circles around her pebbled nipple as my hand dipped down between her legs.

She gasped as my finger glided across her slit and then went inside of her. Her pussy was so wet that my finger easily slipped in, followed by another. I continued to lick and tease her nipples, taking my time to suck them with just enough pressure to get the moan out of her that I wanted. She clenched her thighs in response, and I felt her get wetter.

I grinned as I enjoyed the way her body was reacting to me. Slowly, I worked my way down and parted her thighs with my head before pulling my fingers out. Once she was fully opened, I licked her slit, sucking up the trail of wetness before plunging my tongue inside of her. She gasped again, this time, reaching down to hold my head in place as she ground her hips to get the friction that she needed.

I moved up, focusing my mouth on her clit as I sucked, teasing it in circular motions with my tongue. I could feel her body tightening around me and knew that she was on the verge. I kept going, sucking hard as she pulled my hair and let out a moan that was much louder—and sexier than I had heard before with the food. I felt her pussy spasm around my fingers, taking satisfaction knowing that I was responsible for that orgasm.

"Tanner," she panted heavily. "Tanner, I need you inside of me."

"I'm coming, baby," I whispered, moving up her body before reaching over to the nightstand to grab a condom. "Roll over," I commanded, as I slid the sheath over my dick.

She did as asked and got on her hands and knees with her ass facing me. Everything about her was perfect, from the perfectly round globes of her ass to the tight pussy that was waiting for me. I reached down and held onto her hip, keeping her in place as I slid myself inside of her.

"Fuck," she moaned and instantly started moving her hips against me.

"You got that right," I growled, holding her hips as I drove into her from behind. I wasn't sure how she wanted it, or what she was into, but I knew that this position had the opportunity for another orgasm, and I wanted to feel her come on my cock.

"Harder," she begged, pushing her ass into me. "Please, give it to me harder!"

I felt like I was going to explode as I pounded into her in a way that made her moan and cry out every time I did.

"It's—oh my God. Oh my God!" she cried and spread her legs further. "It's too much pressure, I'm gonna come again!"

"Come for me, Gen," I coaxed. "I want to feel your pussy clench around my cock, draining it. Come on, baby, give me that orgasm."

"I—I—I can't!" she cried, and then I felt her body give in as she spasmed around me. "Oh my God! Tanner! Tanner! Tanner!" she screamed breathlessly.

I kept thrusting, my orgasm close behind hers. I pumped harder and faster, ropes of cum shooting into the condom as I tried to catch my breath. Once I was done, I paused for a moment to catch my breath, gently rubbing my hands up and down her back soothingly.

I pulled out slowly and made sure the condom stayed on. Once I was fully out, she collapsed onto the bed and rolled over. While I was cleaning up my mess, I heard her gasp as she looked down at the wet spot on the bed.

"Did the condom break?" she whispered, her hand covering her mouth in shock.

"No, baby, it didn't break," I assured her, laying down next to her and pulling her over, so she didn't have to be in it.

"Then what happened? What is that?"

I studied her for a quick moment, wondering how old and experienced she really was.

"That's just proof that you had a good orgasm."

"What do you mean?" She pulled her brows in together, confused. "I did that?"

I nodded and leaned down to kiss her forehead.

"I'm so sorry—I don't know how that happened. I'm so embarrassed!"

She pulled her hands up to cover her face.

"Why would you be embarrassed?" I asked, reaching up to pry her hands from her face. "It's sexy to see how turned on you were."

She didn't say anything, just looked at me with uncertainty in her eyes.

"Gen, have you ever had an orgasm like that before?"

She shook her head.

"Not all women are lucky enough to have them, but you seem to react well to having your g-spot stimulated, and that's the orgasm that did that." I nodded to the wet spot without going into any more detail. She laid her head against my chest and rested without saying anything else. My body felt completely spent and relaxed, but my head was flooded with concerns over what I had just done. I knew that we both wanted this tonight, but I couldn't shake the thought that she was more innocent than I had imagined.

Twelve

Gen

What in the world had come over me? I wasn't the kind of girl who just jumped into bed with a man she barely knew, but there was something about Tanner that made me feel oddly comfortable with it. Maybe it was the insane chemistry between us, or perhaps it was the tender way that he was running his fingers up and down the length of my arm as I curled into his side. Either way, I wasn't feeling the pain of regret that I thought for sure would follow my impulsive decision.

"Are you okay?" he asked softly, his lips feathering across my ear and sending shivers through my body.

"I am, thank you. You?"

He let out a deep breath, and my head moved with the rise and fall of his chest. It was such a relaxed movement that I worried we would end up falling asleep soon if we didn't move out of this position. *Was that really such a bad thing?*

"I'm more than good," he confirmed. "I have a beautiful woman lying in my arms after having mind-blowing sex with her. I might even be wonderful at this point," he laughed.

He thought that it was mind-blowing? I knew that *I* thought it was pretty incredible, but I didn't expect him to be so impressed by it. I wasn't a virgin, but I also hadn't been with that many guys, and most of my sexual experience was pretty vanilla, to say the least. To hear that he thought that *I* was mind-blowing was, in fact—blowing my mind.

"I enjoyed it too," I giggled when his hand reached down and grabbed my ass. The feel of his hands on my body again sent a jolt straight to my core, and I started to feel the dull throb between my legs again.

"You might just be the death of me," he teased, letting his hand slip further to where his fingers lined up at my entrance. "But what a way to go."

I closed my eyes and gasped as he parted my legs and slid a finger inside. My body was on fire, and I found that I couldn't get enough of this man. He brought out some wild sex beast that I didn't know was inside of me, and it was ready to get its fill of him.

An hour later, we were both sweaty and tired, sprawled out naked on his bed. The snow had already gotten worse outside, with the storm moving in quickly. I glanced at my phone and cringed when I realized that it was already after ten o'clock, and I didn't want to have to ask Parker or Sheila to come pick me up this late, especially in this weather.

"You can stay the night," he offered as if reading my thoughts.

I clutched my phone to my chest and considered it.

"I don't want to inconvenience you. I can call and ask someone to come pick me up." I felt stupid for not insisting that I drive myself over, but it didn't matter at this point—I was already here without my car, so I had to make a decision.

"It's not an inconvenience at all. I wouldn't have offered if I didn't mean it. I may be from LA, but that doesn't mean that I can't drive in this storm," he laughed. "If you'd rather go home, I'm more than happy to take you, but like I said, you're welcome to stay here if you'd like. No pressure either way."

"Are you sure?" I asked, biting my bottom lip.

He didn't say anything, just arched a brow at me and smirked as if he already knew that I wanted to stay.

"I'm just going to call Sheila real quick, so she doesn't worry," I said nervously, still holding my phone against me.

"Take your time. I'll give you some space," he replied, getting up from the bed and tugging on his boxer briefs. "I'll be in the living room."

I nodded and waited until he left before I sat on the edge of the bed and called Sheila. I chewed my nail while I waited for her to answer, wondering if it was too late and I was waking her up.

On the fifth ring, she answered, sounding out of breath and winded.

"Hey, everything okay?" I asked, hoping that she didn't sound that way because she was doing what I had spent most of my night doing.

"Yeah," she huffed. "I'm fine. Sally's hamster got loose, and I was chasing it through the living room. That little fucker is fast."

I covered my mouth to try to keep from laughing.

"How's your night going?" she asked, ignoring my chuckle on the other line.

"It's good," I said slowly, deciding how much to tell her. "*Really* good."

"Does that mean what I think it means?"

"It does," I giggled. "I don't know what's gotten into me!"

"I would say *who*," she teased. "But we already know the answer to that one."

I laughed and laid back on the bed, memories of his body on top of mine playing in my head as goosebumps spread across my skin. I had thrown on a t-shirt that he gave me, but aside from that, I was still completely naked.

"So, how was it?" Sheila asked.

"Great. Wonderful. Fantastic." I paused and let out a heavy sigh. "I can't even begin to describe it."

"It sounds like you're having a good time, especially given how late it is," she teased.

"About that," I said, feeling nervous all of a sudden. "I was calling to let you know that I won't be back tonight. I didn't want you guys—mainly Parker—to worry."

"You're staying the night?!"

I could hear the excitement in her voice, and it sent another rush of giddiness through me.

"Yeah, he asked if I wanted to."

"I'm really happy for you, Gen. Call me if you need anything, and be sure to use protection. You know what happens if you don't," she joked.

"Don't worry, I've learned a few tricks from Megan. I'll be taking mine *and* yours, just to be on the safe side."

She laughed, the sound pulling a smile across my face.

"Well, Lord knows that I don't need them anymore. Go have fun, and I'll talk to you tomorrow."

"Okay, good night. And please don't tell my dad that I'm spending the night at some guy's house that I don't know." I winced at the thought of having to see him tomorrow and having him know why I didn't come home tonight.

"What am I supposed to tell him?"

"I don't know?" I paused for a moment. "That I'm sleeping over at a friend's house?"

"Do you really think he's going to believe that?"

I groaned, knowing that he wouldn't. I hadn't spent nearly enough time in Stone Creek to make any friends, and I purposely kept it that way because I knew that I wouldn't be staying.

"No, but it sure beats the—your daughter was whoring it up last night with some sexy stranger that she barely knew before she climbed into bed with him."

There was silence on the other end, and I had to pull my phone away from my ear to make sure she hadn't hung up on me.

"Okay, you're right. I'll think of a lie of some sort. Maybe I'll be lucky, and he'll already be asleep."

"Or you could just distract him so he doesn't realize that I'm not home, and I'll sneak back in the morning?"

"I'm going to pretend that I didn't hear you just say that," she pretended to scold.

"What? It's not like it wouldn't work? Plus, you would get something out of it too," I joked, hinting at the possibility of her having some alone time with him.

"No, I'm going to pretend that I didn't hear you because I'm a terrible liar, and your dad will know something is off if I try. So go, have fun, and try to be back before he gets up in the morning."

"Deal," I laughed.

It felt nice talking to Sheila about things, even if it reminded me of my conversations with my mom when she was still alive.

I put my phone down on the dresser and made my way into the living room, where I found Tanner sitting on the couch, watching the sports channel.

"Hey," he said when he noticed me walk in. "Everything okay?"

"Yeah, I just let Sheila know that I wouldn't be back tonight, so they didn't worry or try to come look for me in this storm."

"That was very considerate of you. I'm sure she appreciates it."

I smiled, unsure of what to say or do. Part of me wanted to go curl up next to him again, but then I worried that I would be overstepping. We weren't dating, just two people on a date that were having A LOT of sex.

"Since you're staying over, did you want another glass of wine?" he asked, turning off the tv and standing up.

"Sure, that sounds nice. Thank you."

I followed him into the kitchen and sat down on the padded stool at the island, watching as he grabbed two clean glasses from the cabinet before reaching into the fridge for the bottle of wine. The muscles in his back tightened and flexed as he moved around without a shirt to obscure my view. My fingers itched to reach over and touch him, to trace circles along every inch of his beautifully toned body.

It was pretty unfair that he was this gorgeous, nice, *and* a doctor on top of everything else. He was like this perfect package of sexiness that I couldn't wait to unwrap.

He uncorked the wine, the soft pop sounding more erotic than it should have been. Just being near him was enough to make every nerve stand on end and had my body begging for his touch. He filled both glasses and handed me one, a sexy smirk painted on his gorgeous face as if he knew what I had been thinking.

"Do you want dessert?" he asked, raising his eyebrows.

"Is that a trick question?" I replied, wondering if he was hinting at another round in the bedroom. In that case—yes, I definitely wanted dessert, and my appetite was getting bigger by the second.

He chuckled and opened the freezer, pulling out a carton of ice cream and setting it on the island beside me. Next, he grabbed a can of whipped cream and some hot fudge and added them to the pile he had started. He opened the hot fudge and scooped some into a bowl before popping it into the microwave. A few seconds later, he took it out, testing the warmth with his finger as he stirred it around.

"Do you like hot fudge?" he asked, his voice low and gravely again.

I nodded, watching him as he crossed the room and stood in front of me. He set the bowl down next to me and turned me on the stool, so I was facing him.

"Take off your shirt," he commanded, the growing bulge in his boxers hinting at his arousal.

I didn't take my eyes off of him as I reached down and grabbed the bottom, pulling it over my head and tossing it to the floor beside me. I shivered as I sat naked in front of him, his eyes roaming over every inch of my body.

He pulled his lower lip in between his teeth, his eyes locking onto mine. He reached over and dipped his finger into the hot fudge, then slowly rubbed it across my nipple. I gasped at the sensation from the heat on my skin to the feeling of his wet tongue as he leaned forward and licked it off. My fingers wrapped in his hair, holding him closer as he sucked harder.

My eyes were closed as he added more to the other nipple before continuing with his deliciously brutal torture. My back arched, and my legs spread as I made room for him between my legs while he sucked the thick fudge from my breasts. It was pure ecstasy, and I already felt like I needed him again. I was panting, clawing at his back as he chuckled against my neck.

"I thought you asked if *I* wanted dessert," I teased, grabbing his head and holding it in front of mine. "You don't share very well, now do you?"

"What did you have in mind?" he asked, his grey eyes darkening.

I licked my lips, suddenly feeling braver and more confident than before. I gently pushed him away and got up from the barstool, reaching for the can of whipped cream.

"Drop them," I demanded, nodding to his underwear that was barely containing the massive hard-on.

He smiled a crooked smile and raised an eyebrow as he hooked his fingers in the waistband and did as I asked. I watched wide-eyed as his cock sprung free, ready for me to have my way with it.

I shook the can and kept my eyes locked on his as I kneeled before him. With a quick flick, the cap was off, and I was spraying a line of whipped cream along the length of his dick, watching as his body reacted to the cold sensation. I set the can beside me and leaned forward, slowly licking it off.

I swirled my tongue lazily around his length, satisfied with the change in his breathing as he got more aroused. Once the whipped cream was off, I looked up and smiled as he watched me take him into my mouth. I relaxed my jaw and leaned forward, taking as much of his cock in as I could. He gasped as his hand grabbed the back of my head, working me to the rhythm that he liked as my head bobbed back and forth quickly. I reached down and gently caressed his balls with one hand while the other hand stroked him where my mouth didn't reach.

"Fuck, Gen," he panted, his body stiffening around me.

I flattened my tongue and sucked harder, getting wetter as I felt his body react to me. I was about to get off from making him come, which only spurred me on even more. I let go and used both hands to grab his ass, forcing him to fuck my face as I sucked harder. I could tell by his breathing that it wasn't going to be long before he came.

"I'm gonna come," he warned, giving me time to pull away. Instead, I wrapped my mouth tighter around him and kept going until I felt the salty liquid hit the back of my throat in rapid bursts. Once he was finished, I pulled away and wiped my mouth with my fingers before taking his hand as he helped me up.

"That was fucking incredible," he murmured as he wrapped his arms around my waist and pulled me close to him. "I don't think I'm going to be able to stop fucking you tonight."

"Good, because I don't want you to."

He let out a low growl in my ear before lifting me over his shoulder and grabbing my ass cheeks before leading me back to the bedroom.

"Wait! We forgot the ice cream," I yelped, giggling when his hand slapped my ass.

"I'll buy more," he said sexily. "Right now, I want you again."

Thirteen

Tanner

I was exhausted. Absolutely, completely exhausted to the point that I couldn't find the energy to lift my arm and turn off the tv after Gen fell asleep in my arms. I wasn't eighteen anymore—that was for damn sure. But I was still pleased that I had the stamina to keep me going after our insane night of constant fucking.

No matter how hard I tried, I couldn't keep my hands off of her. But the best part about it—she couldn't resist me either. There was this strong pull between us that neither of us were willing to fight. Maybe it was because it felt so damn good to just give in and enjoy each other.

It was after two in the morning by the time we gave in and went to sleep. When I woke up in the morning, I was surprised to find the bed empty with only a note beside me. I groaned and ran a hand over my face before reading it, already knowing what it was going to say.

I picked it up and let out a sigh before reading it.

Tanner, after depriving me of ice cream last night, I felt it was only fair to make you pay. I have commandeered your bathtub and do not plan to give it back until my skin is more wrinkled than a raisin.

I felt my cheeks split, as the laugh bellowed out of me. I tossed the note on the bed and jumped up, hoping to catch her before she got out. I made a quick pit stop in the guest bathroom before knocking on the door to the master bath.

"I'm not a raisin yet," she teased from the other side. "I refuse to get out before then."

I laughed and opened the door, leaning against the frame as I took in the beautiful sight before me.

The large soaking tub was filled to the top with bubbles while Gen relaxed beneath them, her hair pulled up into a messy bun. I could barely see the top of her breasts under all of the bubbles and found myself yearning for more.

"I won't kick you out," I said, licking my lips. "But that doesn't mean that I won't come join you."

A flash of desire streaked across her face as she scooted forward and smiled. I pulled off my briefs and kicked them to the side, wondering how much more my dick could take. I hadn't had this much sex since I was a teenager, and I was already in my thirties. A lot had changed over the years, but apparently, Gen was the secret to keeping my dick young.

I climbed in behind her, laughing when some of the water sloshed over the side from the movement as the water raised around us. Once I was situated, I wrapped my arm around her waist and pulled her back against my chest.

It was still early in the morning, barely after seven, but I didn't know what time she was planning to leave. It was an odd feeling, but deep down, I hoped that it wasn't any time soon. It wasn't just the constant physical interaction between us, but I really did enjoy her company and found that I wanted to spend more time getting to know her.

"Do you have any plans today?" I asked, hoping to sound as carefree as possible.

"You mean other than forcing myself into your tub and refusing to leave until I'm a raisin?" she joked, tilting her head to look at me. "That was all that I had planned."

"Good," I whispered. "Because I was hoping that maybe we could spend more time together. Get to know each other better."

She giggled as I ran my hand up her thigh and kissed her neck. Thirty minutes later, we were both full raisin status, and the water was cold. I offered her a pair of my sweats and a t-shirt, so she didn't have to wear the same clothes as last night, but I had to admit that it made my dick hard thinking about her not wearing any panties.

I was just about to ask what she wanted to do today when her phone rang. Her eyes widened, and she chewed her nail as she debated whether to answer.

"It's Sheila," she said, looking up at me. "I probably need to take this since I told her that I would be home this morning."

I nodded and turned my back, trying to give her privacy as I got dressed.

"Hey," she answered.

I bent down and pulled my shoes on when I heard the change in her tone.

"Sheila, what's wrong? Are you okay?" She hesitated for a moment, then looked at me with panic in her eyes. "Yeah, he's right here."

She held the phone to her chest and spoke in a hushed tone.

"Something's wrong with the baby."

I pinched my brows together and took the phone as she handed it to me.

"Hey, Sheila, what's going on?"

"I'm so sorry to bother you," she said, crying. "I think something is wrong. I woke up bleeding."

"It's okay, you're not bothering at all. How much blood?"

"Not a lot. It was on the sheets, I didn't notice it until I came back from using the restroom. It was still dark, so I didn't notice if there was any blood when I peed." She hesitated for a moment. "I'm really scared that something is wrong.

I'm not through the first trimester yet, and I know that—"

"Hey, let's not think the worst right now, okay?" I rushed to assure her. "Can you meet me at the clinic in fifteen minutes?"

"Yes."

"Okay, I'm heading there now. Do you have someone that can take you, or do you need me to stop and pick you up?"

"I'll have Parker drive. We'll be there soon."

I let out a deep breath and handed Gen back her phone after Sheila hung up.

"Is she okay?" she asked nervously.

"I won't know much until I can examine her at the clinic. I'll do an ultrasound, and we should have some answers then."

I grabbed my phone and keys from the nightstand and tried to calm my own nerves.

"Are you ready?"

She nodded, and we rushed out the door. The snow was still falling as we drove to the clinic. It was hard not to speed because I felt the urgency talking to Sheila, but I also didn't want to risk us getting in an accident on the way because of the weather.

By the time we got there, there was another car waiting in

the parking lot. We got out, and I rushed over to open Gen's door, feeling the penetrating glare from the man with Sheila.

"How are you feeling?" I asked Sheila over my shoulder as I unlocked the door. I pushed it open and stepped to the side, letting them through before I pulled it closed and locked it.

"I'm okay, just a little sore and have some mild cramping."

I tried to keep the frown off my face as I walked us down the hallway to the first exam room. I turned on the light and opened the drawer where the gowns were kept.

"Go ahead and get undressed from the waist down, and I'll be back in a minute to check you," I said, handing her the gown.

I walked out and closed the door behind us as Gen stepped out with me.

"I'm so worried," she admitted shyly, wrapping her arms around herself. She looked so small in my clothes as they hung loosely around her body.

"It'll be okay," I assured her, pulling her in for a hug. It felt nice to hold her against me, and I wanted to stay in that moment forever.

Suddenly, the door opened, and I was greeted with a frown as Parker's dark green eyes studied us.

"She's ready."

I sucked in a deep breath and followed Gen inside.

"Do you want me to wait outside?" Gen asked her, standing by the bed.

"No, you're fine to stay," Sheila said, squeezing her hand. "This is Parker, by the way," she added, nodding to him as I sat down on the stool in front of the bed and pulled on a pair of latex gloves. "He's my boyfriend, and he's also Gen's dad."

I tried to keep the shock off of my face as the news hit me like a ton of bricks. No wonder this guy was shooting daggers at me every chance he got. It had nothing to do with Sheila but everything to do with him seeing me embrace his daughter in the hallway *after* showing up with her in my car.

"It's a pleasure to meet you," I said calmly, offering him the most professional smile that I could muster. When he didn't say anything in return, I decided to go about my business. He stood there scowling, arms folded over his chest as if he didn't trust me. In all fairness, I couldn't say that I blamed him, given how we were meeting for the first time.

I did a quick exam before pulling off the gloves and turning on the computer to do the ultrasound.

"Everything looks fine," I said as I typed in my password. "Your cervix is fully closed, and I didn't see any signs of bleeding. We'll get a better look with the ultrasound," I continued as I handed her the wand to insert inside of herself. Once it was situated, I took it from her and gently moved it around until I got the image I was trying to find.

I leaned forward and studied the screen, making sure I wasn't missing anything.

"The baby looks great," I confirmed, smiling over my shoulder at her before returning my attention to the screen. "I don't see anything that concerns me."

"That's great news," Gen said, relieved.

"Thank you, Doctor Hayes. I appreciate you taking the time to come down here and check me."

"It's not a problem at all," I replied, leaning forward to turn the audio on. "Here's the baby's heartbeat. Nice and strong."

I held the wand in place and turned around, watching as Parker's stone-cold expression changed the second he heard it. His eyes grew bigger, and his arms dropped as he stepped closer to Sheila and looked back and forth between the screen and her stomach.

"That's our baby?" he whispered. She nodded as a tear slid down her cheek.

"That's our baby."

I didn't want to interrupt this moment, so I held the wand for a few more minutes, allowing them this opportunity to bond over this blessing. I glanced up at Gen, who had tears of her own dotting the corners of her eyes.

I looked away, giving them their privacy before turning off the sound and pulling the wand out. Once she was situated, I turned my attention back to her.

"Everything looks fine," I repeated. "The bleeding could have been from a number of things— cervical changes, intercourse—" I was about to go on when I noticed the blush creep up her face as she looked away.

I cleared my throat before continuing.

"Sex during pregnancy is safe and can cause bleeding during the first trimester. Since the bleeding has stopped, I would recommend drinking plenty of water and resting if it helps put your mind at ease."

"Thanks, Doctor Hayes," Sheila said sheepishly.

"See, I told you we shouldn't have done that," Parker whispered, not realizing that it was loud enough to hear.

A phone started ringing, and Parker reached into his pocket to get it.

"It's Ryder," he said to Sheila before going to the hallway to answer it.

Once the door clicked shut, I focused on entering my notes in the system from the unexpected visit.

"Sheila!" Gen blurted out quietly.

"What? You told me to distract him, so I did."

I coughed to hide the chuckle that was trying to force its way out.

"Why didn't you just put on Titanic? You know that movie always puts him to sleep."

"Because he was getting all antsy, asking where you were.

Ryder had texted him about you being on a date with the hot new doctor in town, and he started to get all worked up. It was either that or have him come looking for you in the middle of the night during this crazy storm. Plus, it was a nice distraction if I do say so myself," Sheila teased.

"Eww. Yuck."

"Don't be such a prude," Sheila joked.

If she only knew how sexual Gen was, she wouldn't think she was a prude at all.

"It's my dad," she whined. "It's always going to be gross."

I decided that was my cue to interrupt and stop the conversation from getting any worse. I tore the ultrasound pictures off the printer and handed them to Sheila.

"You're all set to go, I'll step out so you can get dressed."

"Thank you, and again, I'm really sorry for dragging you down here. Can I make it up to you by having you over for dinner? I make a killer meatloaf…."

I glanced at Gen, trying to gauge her reaction but couldn't read it.

"Please, I just feel terrible."

"I'm not sure that Parker would love the idea, but thank you so much for the offer. Really, you don't owe me anything. I was just doing my job."

"Parker will be fine with it," Sheila said happily as the door opened and he walked in, another frown on his face.

"I'll be fine with what?"

"Doctor Hayes is joining us for dinner tonight," Sheila announced matter-of-factly.

I raised my eyebrows at Gen, desperate for her to say something if she didn't want me to come over. Instead, she just smiled then turned to look at her dad with a worried look on her face.

And just like that, I was meeting her family and going over for dinner.

98

Fourteen

Gen

"Are you sure this is a good idea?" I asked Sheila as she pulled the meatloaf out of the oven and set it on the stove.

I had spent the day at home, trying to get a feel for how Parker was handling the news that I was dating the man who was also his girlfriend's gynecologist. I really wanted to spend it with Tanner, but things felt awkward when we got ready to leave the clinic, so I went ahead and grabbed a ride back with Sheila and ensured Tanner that he didn't have to come to dinner.

We had texted a few times throughout the day, and he promised that he would *discreetly* bring my clothes back from last night and that he was looking forward to dinner tonight. Sheila had also *conveniently* arranged for the kids to stay the night with her parents tonight, so it was just the four of us for dinner.

"Too late to back out now," she laughed as the doorbell rang. "Can you go grab that?"

I sucked in a deep breath and adjusted my sweater that suddenly felt too tight as I headed toward the door. Thankfully, Parker was in the bathroom, which gave me a few minutes to talk to Tanner without him hovering or overhearing our conversation.

"Hey," I said, opening the door and stepping to the side. "How are you?"

"I'm good, how are you?" he asked, sliding his hand around my waist to my back as he gave me a quick kiss.

"Nervous," I admitted, feeling my emotions getting the better of me.

"Me too," he laughed, handing me the bottle of wine that he brought. "Liquid courage," he shrugged and raised his eyebrows.

I shook my head and smiled, suddenly feeling more relaxed. I could still feel the heat from his fingers and missed his touch.

"Come on inside," I invited, leading him through the living room to the kitchen.

"Tanner brought wine," I announced, handing it to Sheila as she turned around. Her face was beaming with a smile that hurt my face from how tight it stretched across hers.

"Thank you so much, that was very sweet of you. Dinner

will be ready in a few minutes, go ahead and have a seat."

We sat on one side of the table, the uneasiness steadily starting to creep back in. A few minutes later, Parker came in and forced a smile as he saw Tanner sitting beside me.

"Doctor Hayes," he said as he extended his hand to shake. Tanner stood up and took it, smiling the same tight smile that I had seen earlier.

"Please, call me Tanner," he insisted, sitting down.

Parker nodded but didn't say anything as he walked over and wrapped his arms around Sheila's waist, whispering something in her ear. She giggled and swatted at him.

"Make yourself useful and take the mashed potatoes to the table, please," she said with a teasing tone.

"Yes, ma'am," he joked, reaching around her to grab the bowl.

She joined us a few minutes later after bringing over the meatloaf, some freshly baked rolls, and the tub of butter. Once she was sure that we had everything we needed, she took her seat beside Parker.

"Everything smells delicious," Tanner said, giving her the smile that made my knees weak. "Thank you again for the invite."

"It's our pleasure. Now let's eat before it gets cold." Sheila smiled and gently nudged Parker in the side.

"Would you like a beer, Tanner?" he asked, his voice hoarse as if it pained him to ask.

"Sure, thank you."

"Gen?" He gave me a look I had seen him use plenty of times with the kids and had to fight back the laugh. I was twenty-two years old and had drunk with them plenty of times over the past year.

"No, thank you," I said with a light laugh. "I think I'll have some of the wine that Tanner brought since Sheila can't partake."

We got our drinks and got settled again, silence falling around us as we ate. Sheila didn't lie—her meatloaf was amazing, and I found myself wanting to eat seconds because it was so good. My stomach was already tight from being overly full.

I helped clean up the dishes and kicked Sheila out to go rest while Tanner helped me. It was nice having a few minutes by ourselves.

"It's not as bad as you thought it would be, is it?" he asked quietly, standing next to me as he dried the dishes that I handed him. We had already loaded most of them into the dishwasher except for the few that were too big and needed to be hand washed.

"Honestly, I didn't know what to expect. Parker wasn't around much when I was growing up, so I didn't have those experiences with him when I started dating. We're still trying to figure out our relationship, but I think it's hard for him to see me with you."

"Because I'm so much older?"

"I don't know," I answered honestly. "Maybe that, or possibly because you're his wife's doctor and you're sleeping with his daughter. It could be a combination of things."

He didn't respond right away, he just furrowed his brow as he thought about something.

"Does it bother you that I'm older than you?"

I turned the water off and shifted to look at him.

"No. Does it bother you?"

He shook his head, but it wasn't a clear enough answer for me.

"It doesn't bother me, but I worry that you're so young and innocent, and here I am, corrupting you."

I let out a laugh, unable to control myself.

"Trust me, I don't think you're corrupting me. I haven't done anything that I didn't want to."

Which was true. Everything that we'd done were things that I wanted, and even though I wasn't as experienced, I didn't regret doing them. It was like he was liberating a side of me that I didn't know was locked up.

"You're still innocent, aren't you?"

"Are you asking if I was a virgin before we had sex?" I asked, confused.

He waited, struggling with what to say.

"No, Tanner. I wasn't a virgin. I had been with a few guys before you, I just didn't experiment much when I was with them. Sex isn't new to me, just the other stuff that we did. Which I happened to like a lot, by the way."

"I never want to take advantage," he replied quietly.

"You're not," I assured him, rubbing my hand soothingly up and down his arm.

"I don't think everyone feels the same way," he muttered, glancing into the living room before going back to drying the dishes.

I looked past him and found Parker sitting on the couch with Sheila's legs draped over him, scowling at us.

Fifteen

Tanner

Dinner wasn't as awkward as I thought it would be, and by the end, I was hopeful that I had started to win Parker over some with our shared love for the Tennessee Titans. I'd never been much of a sports fan, but I found that moving to a small town meant that I needed to pick a team— and quickly. Stone Creek just happened to love football, even though I never really understood why people loved the sport so much.

I helped Gen clean after we were all done and took my cue to leave before Sheila insisted that I stay and hang out a bit. I could tell by the way Parker was working his jaw back and forth that he wasn't fond of having me there. The tension in the room grew thick when we didn't have much to talk about.

"So, Tanner," Sheila said, redirecting the conversation for what felt like the fiftieth time in an hour. "What made you decide to come to Stone Creek?"

I hated this question and usually sidestepped around it with some vague response, but for whatever reason, I decided to open up to them.

"My mom," I said, looking down at the beer bottle in my hands as I rested my elbows on my knees.

"Is she from here?"

I looked at Gen then turned my attention to Sheila, pulling my shoulders back as I sat taller.

"No, we have no connections to Tennessee whatsoever. She grew up in a small town and lived there her entire life. Once I graduated high school, I couldn't wait to get the hell out of there and move to a big city. I got a full-ride scholarship to Stanford and then put myself through medical school. I did my residency in Los Angeles and decided that I wanted to make more of a difference, so I ventured down the small town path and ended up here."

Okay, so it wasn't the full details that I could have shared, but I didn't want to depress everyone with my sob story.

"What made you decide to go small town?" Sheila prodded.

I leaned back against the couch and felt Gen's hand brush against mine. She smiled softly as she waited to hear the rest of my story.

"My mom got sick and didn't tell me until it was too late. Since she lived in a small town, she didn't have the same resources available to her that she would have if she were in a big city. By the time I found out, it was too late. There wasn't anything that I could do to help her. The cancer had already spread through her body at that point."

"I'm so sorry," Gen whispered quietly beside me.

"What kind of cancer?" Parker asked, surprising me.

"It started as cervical cancer. It showed on early scans when she started to feel sick, but her doctor didn't catch it. She could have had a complete hysterectomy and would likely have survived it, but by the time they caught it, it had already metastasized through her body."

I felt Gen's body trembling beside me and looked to find her crying. I wrapped my arm around her and held her, rubbing her back softly.

"Gen lost her mom a few months ago," Sheila explained quietly. "I'm sorry for your loss, Tanner."

"Thank you," I sighed heavily, still comforting Gen. "After she passed, I decided that I didn't care about the money or working for some prestigious hospital. I switched my specialty and decided to find a small town and do something good with my knowledge and skills. Give them the resources that I wish my mom had."

"It's a touching story," Parker said, the gruff in his voice finally subsiding. "We're lucky to have you as Sheila's doctor."

"I'm happy to do what I can while I'm here."

Gen wiped the tears from her face and pulled away, looking at me through the tears that were still flooding her eyes.

"Are you not staying in Stone Creek for long?" she asked, sniffling.

"It's a temporary job, six months at most. From there, we'll see what town I end up in next."

"So you're not staying here?"

I felt the tension in the room thicken again.

"No, that was never the plan," I said softly, noticing the hurt in her eyes.

"Well, it's getting late, so I'm going to head to bed," Parker said, breaking the silence that had fallen over the room. He stood up and stretched before extending a hand to help Sheila off the couch next to him.

"Yeah, me too," she said, playing along with his excuse to give us some privacy. "Goodnight, you guys. Thanks again for your help this morning, Tanner."

"No problem," I said, giving them a quick wave as they headed toward the hallway. "Thank you for dinner, it was delicious."

Sheila tossed a *you're welcome* over her shoulder as Parker led her to their room.

Once we were alone, I turned to look at Gen. She was still crying, her face red and splotchy as she blew her nose into a tissue.

"Are you okay?" I asked, gently rubbing my hand on her knee.

"I'm fine," she lied, sucking in a jagged breath. "It's not like this was anything serious. I was planning to leave soon anyway, so why does it matter that you are too?"

I felt the pain in my stomach as I realized what she was really upset about. And just like that, we had crossed a line we hadn't even seen until now.

Sixteen

Gen

"Good morning," Parker said from the kitchen table, reading the newspaper as I passed him to get to the coffee.

"Morning," I mumbled, watching the dark liquid fill my cup, reminiscent of how dark my life felt these days. "I'm going out for some fresh air."

I didn't wait for him to say anything or to try to talk me out of it. I knew that it was cold outside and that I would freeze my butt off, but I didn't care. Maybe the cold would match the numbness that I had woken up to.

I opened the backdoor and was surprised to find Sheila sitting at the patio table, wrapped up in a blanket with a coffee cup in her hand.

"It's hot chocolate," she said, lifting her cup. "The doctors say that you can have one cup of coffee a day while you're pregnant, but since we all know that I need a minimum of *four,* I've been sticking with hot chocolate."

"Fair enough," I said, taking the empty seat beside her.

We sat in the cold for a few minutes, sipping our drinks as our teeth chattered from the cold.

"How are you feeling this morning?" she asked, breaking the ice.

I took another drink, trying to figure that out myself.

"I have no idea. I feel stupid for how I acted last night and woke up to a handful of text messages from Tanner, asking if we can talk."

"Why do you feel stupid?"

"Because," I sighed. "I was so upset over hearing that Tanner wasn't staying long—yet, I'm not either. It's crazy, I really don't know what came over me."

Sheila lifted her mug and took another sip.

"Maybe it's because you like him so much?" she offered, holding her cup in front of her face with both hands.

"I barely even know him," I groaned, realizing how childish it sounded. "We had one date and then spent time together yesterday, and I'm acting like he's the love of my life and abandoning me."

"Well, he could be."

"Okay—now you're the one who's being crazy," I laughed, feeling the way my stomach twisted at the idea that I could be in love with someone I hardly knew.

"Maybe. But I knew right away with Parker and look at us now. Sometimes you just feel it and know that you're meant to be with that person. It's hard to describe, but things just fall so easily into place, and everything feels natural that you don't have to struggle to make it work. It just does on its own."

I thought about what she was saying. It was similar to how I felt with Tanner. Everything about him felt easy, and we didn't seem to argue or disagree on much—not that I could really say that given we had spent less than seventy-two hours together. But deep down, I felt like I knew him and that he understood me. It was like we had this connection— both mentally and physically—that I had never experienced with someone else before. The pull between us was so strong, and I couldn't imagine that it was all in my head.

"What if I'm just that desperate to find somewhere to belong that I latch on to the first guy who pays attention to me? So much has changed in the last few months that maybe I'm really just in love with the *idea* of falling in love. Maybe it's just grief mixed in with hormones, and this is all skewing my judgment?"

Sheila set her cup down on the table and turned to look at me, pinning me in place to make sure she had my full attention.

"I know that you've lost so much already, but I hope you know that you will *always* belong here with us. We love and adore you, Gen. You're our family, and I hope you think of us as yours too."

I watched the tears well in her eyes as my throat prickled while I tried to keep mine away.

"I know," I choked out. "I love you guys too. I just don't know where I *belong*. My mom kept telling me to go live my life and be happy, but I don't know what that's supposed to mean. Did she have stuff that she wanted to do and never got around to it? Did she regret having me so young because it kept her from living her life? I feel like there was some sort of a hidden meaning behind her words, and now I'll never know what it was. Maybe I was just clinging to Tanner because he felt fun, and I didn't have to worry about anything else."

"I was eighteen when I had Oliver," she sighed. "Now I look at Megan, pregnant at sixteen and still a baby herself. But when I think back to when I had him, I didn't feel like a child. I felt like an adult, and I knew that I had responsibilities to take care of. My life has been spent raising four kids and making sure that I teach them how to be the best people they can be before releasing them into the world. I don't regret a single day of it, and I can promise you that even if your mom had stuff she wanted to do, there weren't any regrets about having you at a young age and spending her life raising you. It's what we do as parents— it's both a sacrifice and a reward at the same time."

"How am I supposed to know what I want to do with my life? Or what will make me happy?"

"Nobody can answer that but you. But I think you're taking the right steps to try to figure it out. Nothing has to be decided right now, but if you see an opportunity and you want to take it—then go for it. You have plenty of time to decide what you want in life. Right now is about figuring out what makes you happy."

My stomach sank when an image of Tanner flashed through my mind. I hadn't felt this happy in a long time, and I knew it was because of him. It was the little things, like how he would flirt with me and make me blush or when he would say something funny to make me laugh. I hadn't stopped smiling since I first agreed to go on a date with him, and now I felt like I couldn't get that happiness back.

"Being an adult sucks," I muttered, lifting my coffee to take a drink. The cold was starting to settle in my bones, making me shiver.

"It'll get better, just wait and see." She smiled and took another sip of her hot chocolate. We sat there for a few minutes before Parker came out, threatening to carry our stubborn asses in if we didn't get inside where it was warm soon.

I helped Sheila make breakfast, thankful for the quiet while the kids were still at their grandparent's house. I needed time to think and found frying bacon to be oddly satisfying. Once the food was ready, we sat down and joined Parker at the table.

"Everything smells delicious," he said, pulling a napkin out from the holder on the table. "Thank you, ladies, for breakfast."

"You're welcome," Sheila replied, leaning in to give him a quick kiss.

I bit off a piece of bacon, looking down when my phone

vibrated on the table. It was a text message from Tanner, wishing me a good morning. I needed to talk to him about last night, but my head was still a mess. Until I could sort things out on my own, I didn't want to make things more convoluted with him.

"Tanner?" Sheila asked, nodding to my phone. She took a bite of eggs while Parker stayed quiet, his jaw tightening as he took a bite of the sausage link.

"Yeah, he wants to talk."

"That's a good sign," she assured.

"We'll see," I sighed, taking a bite out of my toast.

"Why do you think it's not a good sign?" Parker asked, his tone overly protective. I already knew that he was hoping for this to mean that we were over.

"I didn't say that it's *not* a good sign," I muttered, still feeling irritable with him from yesterday. "I just don't know if there's anything for us to talk about. He's not staying here that long, so why does it matter how we feel about things?"

"In all fairness, you're not planning to stay either," Sheila reminded me.

"I know, I know. It's just already so messy, and things just barely started. I wish I could go back to the other night where we were blissfully unaware of the impending deadline."

The scowl creased harder on Parker's face when I mentioned being with Tanner the other night.

"I'm going to ask you something, and I want you to be completely honest. Give me the first answer that pops into your head." Sheila raised her eyebrows and waited for me to agree.

"Alright, fine."

"*If* Tanner wasn't leaving in a few months, would you stay in Stone Creek to be with him?"

"Yes."

I felt my cheeks flush as my pulse started racing when I realized how easy it was to answer that question without thinking about it.

"Well then, I think you've got the answer that you were looking for."

"What answer? What was the question?" Parker asked, looking between us.

"What makes her happy," Sheila said quietly, giving me a soft smile that told me she knew what I was feeling inside.

The rest of breakfast was uneventful, with Sheila distracting Parker with questions about what he wanted to do for Christmas. His parents had been asking to come in to see them, but he was adamant about keeping them as far away as possible. I ignored the conversation and thought about what I would say to Tanner when I saw him. Once we were finished, I sent him a quick text, asking when we could meet up, and then jumped in the shower.

I got ready quickly, thankful that I didn't have to share the bathroom with anyone else or rush for whoever needed it next. The snow was still coming down heavily, so we agreed to talk at his place. I offered to drive there, so that I didn't have to worry about finding a ride home later, again, but he quickly declined and confirmed he would pick me up in thirty minutes.

My hair was down with loose waves covering the black turtle neck that I needed to hide the few hickies he had accidentally left me. It was soft and comfortable, which was all that mattered at this point. I threw on a pair of comfy, worn-in jeans and did my makeup. It wasn't much, but at least it hid the fact that I cried myself to sleep last night.

I checked my phone, finding a message that he was on his way. I grabbed my stuff and rushed to the front door when Parker stopped me.

"Gen—can we talk for a minute?"

"I'm sorry, Tanner will be here any minute to pick me up."

He ran a hand down his face and sighed.

"I know that I haven't been in your life long enough to have much of a say as your dad, but I don't think you should date him."

I folded my arms over my chest and stared at him.

"Why not?"

"Because," he exhaled. "He's practically ten years older

than you for starters, and two, he doesn't even plan to stay here more than a few months."

"Is that really what's bothering you?" I asked, holding his stare and not backing down.

"Yes, he's too old for you."

"You didn't say anything when I was dating Rodney, and he was even older."

"I didn't know you well enough back then to say something," he gritted out.

"You don't know me well enough now, either."

I could see his temper flaring as my blood ran just as hot.

"That's not fair, Gen. I'm trying and have been since you gave me the opportunity."

"It's not fair of you to tell me who I can and cannot date. He's a good man."

"You don't know that."

"Well, Sheila thinks he's good enough to care for her and the babies," I bit out.

"That's not the same, and you know it."

I heard a car door close and knew he was there.

"It doesn't matter either way. He's here, so I'm leaving. Don't bother waiting up for me tonight."

I didn't wait for his answer as I opened the door and stepped outside.

Tanner was smiling as he walked over, fully decked out in a heavy coat and gloves with a beanie that sat low on his head. He looked like the kind of guy you would see on the cover of an outdoor sports magazine.

"Hey, how are you?" he asked, pulling me in for a hug once we reached each other.

"I've been better," I said, feeling the weight of the fight with my dad sitting on my shoulders.

He pulled back slightly and studied my face, making sure I was okay.

"I'm fine," I rushed out. The last thing that I needed was for him to feel the need to go talk to Parker and get him even more riled up. "Let's get inside the car before we freeze."

Once we got back to Tanner's house, my blood pressure had returned to normal, and I felt terrible for how I had left things at home. I was so mad at my dad that I hadn't even said goodbye to Sheila before I left.

He was busy in the kitchen as I sat on the couch, curled up under a blanket and watching the snow fall outside. It felt calm and peaceful here, and I hated how easy it was to feel at home in his place. A few minutes later, he came and sat beside me on the couch, handing me a cup of hot chocolate with a giant marshmallow floating on top and a thick peppermint stick to stir it with.

"You're the cutest," I said as my cheeks split into a smile. I stirred the hot liquid carefully, feeling like a kid again.

"I'll do whatever it takes to get that smile out of you."

Bonus points.

"Well, I definitely needed one," I admitted.

"Do you want to talk about it?" he asked, setting his cup down on the coffee table to give me his full attention.

I took a deep breath and slowly let it out.

"I got into a fight with my dad right before I left."

"About me?"

I nodded.

"He doesn't want you to see me."

He didn't ask it as a question. It was a statement that I didn't bother to deny.

"I'm sorry," he apologized.

"For what?" I lowered my cup to the table, turning to face him.

"For being the source of conflict between you guys. I know how important family is, and I never want to come between one."

My stomach tightened. I wondered if he was going to use this as his excuse to break things off with me before he left, since things were too complicated.

"My dad is a brilliant man. He's built several businesses from the ground up and has done very well for himself over the years. However, he wasn't around much when I was growing up, so he didn't have a say in what I did or the guys that I dated. Just because we've gotten closer recently doesn't mean that he gets to have one now. I decide what I want and make my own decisions."

He leaned back against the couch and stared at the wall across from us.

"What do you want?"

My palms started sweating when I thought about it.

"You."

His eyes grew wider as he turned to look at me. I could see the questions flashing across his face that he didn't dare speak.

"I know that we haven't known each other very long, and maybe I'm feeling something that you're not," I blurted out quickly, hoping that I hadn't scared him with my confession.

He held his hand up to stop me as he grinned the cheeky smile that I loved.

"I want you too, Gen."

Seventeen

Tanner

It felt good to have Gen laying in my arms again. After not getting a response back from my texts last night, I was worried that I had ruined things between us before they had a chance to start. I had spent most of my night staring at my phone, willing it to ring, and was exhausted this morning.

"So," she said quietly, her cheek pressed against my chest. "We've done well with avoiding the elephant in the room, but I need to know—how long are you here for?"

I knew that we would have to talk about it sooner rather than later, but I had been trying to postpone it as long as possible after her reaction to it last night.

"Doctor Long and I have an agreement to discuss my position after New Year's. We'll sit down and see whether this is a good fit for her practice, and whether this is something that I want to make a longer commitment to."

"How do you feel about it so far?"

"Honestly," I sighed. "I don't know. It's only been a week, but I'm already starting to remember why I left small-town life to begin with," I laughed.

"Is it really that bad?" she asked quietly.

I paused and thought about it.

"Not bad, just different. I'm used to doing what I want without having to worry about other people talking about it. Here, everyone knows my business whether I want them to or not."

"I get that. I lived in Nashville when I was going to school, and it's definitely different than the small town I grew up in."

"So, what about you? How long are you planning to stay in Stone Creek?"

She squirmed in my arms, and I felt the way her body stiffened.

"I'm not sure. I haven't really given it much thought yet."

"Do you think you'll end up staying here after all?"

"It's a possibility."

She shrugged and laced her fingers between mine as she laid against my chest. I couldn't see her face from this angle, so I had no idea if she was upset. She was quiet and didn't offer much other than that, so I decided to change the subject.

"Are you going to be in town for the big carnival thing?" I asked, not remembering what it was called. All that I knew was that it was a big event in Stone Creek, and several of the locals had already asked if I was going.

"The Winter Fair?" she asked, turning her head to look at me.

"Yeah, that's it," I laughed. "I couldn't remember the name of it, which is surprising given how much everyone has talked about it."

"I plan to be here for it. I promised Sally that she could take me and show me around since it'll be my first one."

"Sally is your sister?" I asked, trying to remember the siblings' names she had told me about the other night.

"I consider her my sister, but she's Sheila's daughter with her ex-husband, Rodney."

"The guy you were engaged to?" I pulled my brows together, remembering the jealousy that had washed over me when I had heard about that from Dottie a few days after I had told her to stop gossiping about people.

"How did you hear about that?" she asked, shocked that I knew.

"Small towns," I chuckled. "Nothing stays a secret for long."

"Ain't that the truth," she grumbled. "But yes, Rodney was my fiancé. I met him while I lived in Nashville, but I didn't know the crazy little love triangle that was going to unfold. I had just gotten in touch with my dad again while he lived in Nashville and had no idea that he was dating Sheila or that she was Rodney's ex-wife."

"What made you guys decide not to get married?"

"Once I met Sheila and saw what a wonderful person she is, it shifted the way that I saw Rodney. I didn't want to get in the middle of it, and I found myself taking her side when it came to the kids. Then, I realized that he wasn't what I wanted after all. He was way too old for me, and we were just at different points in our lives."

"How do you feel about our age difference?" I asked cautiously, rubbing my finger lightly up and down her arm.

"Honestly, I don't have a problem with it. You're not that much older than I am, and I feel like we're more on the same page than I ever was with Rodney."

"I'm thirty-two, Gen. You're barely twenty—" I left off the rest of the sentence, realizing that I didn't know how old she is. I had only guessed that she was in her early twenties.

"Twenty-two," she finished for me. "But I'm turning twenty-three in January."

"Still, there's a ten-year age difference between us. That doesn't bother you?"

"Should it?" She sat up and turned to face me, crossing her legs into a pretzel as she sat on the other side of the bed.

"No," I sighed. "I just wanted to make sure that you knew how old I was."

"Well, now that we've got the important things settled, why don't we stop talking and do something that we both want?"

I watched her crawl across the bed, her dark eyes clouded with desire as she climbed on top of me and pinned my back to the bed.

"And what's that?" I asked, knowing full well what she had in mind as my dick hardened beneath her.

"I'll give you a hint," she whispered, pulling my t-shirt that I loaned her up and over her head before tossing it behind her. She leaned down and kissed me, her naked breasts warm on my chest as her nipples puckered from the cold.

She slid down my body, still straddling me, and pulled off my sweats and boxer shorts, letting my erection spring free. Her hand gripped it firmly, stroking it up and down as she locked eyes with me and licked her lips. Slowly, she lowered her head and took my length in her mouth, opening her jaw to accommodate as much as she could. She started slow, her tongue swirling in circles around the head while her hand tightened around me as she pumped faster.

I closed my eyes and relished in the sensations running through me as her beautiful mouth sucked me hard and fast. I was on the verge of climax, but the only thing that was running through my mind was that I needed to slow things down between us before one of us got hurt.

Eighteen

Gen

The last few weeks had flown by faster than I had realized. Sean had called to let me know that they were officially moving to Alabama to be with his family in March and asked if I had changed my mind about coming with them. When I declined, he made sure to let me know that I had some time to get my stuff from the house and to go through my mom's things before he packed any of it up. It was another piece of the puzzle that I wasn't ready for, but I knew that I had to get that closure at some point.

Tanner and I had been seeing each other almost every day, and I stayed at his house most nights—much to the irritation of Parker. I had hoped that by being in Stone Creek, our relationship would get stronger, but it seemed that my choice in men only made it harder. I loved my dad, but I hated that he wouldn't give Tanner a chance to show him what a good man he was and how much he cared about me. We had been technically dating for three weeks, and while that didn't seem like a long time, it felt like one of the best relationships I had ever been in. For once, I was happy again.

"So, are you excited about the Winter Fair?" Brooke asked as I wiped down the counter by the register. I had agreed to help out while Autumn—the girl who has worked for Brooke for years and helps run the place when she's gone—was on vacation in Delaware. Since I was staying in town for a little while, I figured I might as well make some money and fill my time while Tanner was at work.

"I'm looking forward to checking it out. Sally insists that I've never seen anything like it and that I'll be in complete awe the moment I see it."

"Well, she's right. I can assure you that you've never seen anything like it," she laughed. "Whether or not you're in awe, I couldn't say. But, at least it's fun!"

"Are you and Ryder going together?"

"We'll both be working the booth there, but we'll take some time and go walk around like we always do. That's the nice thing about small-town life—I can ask someone to watch our stuff, and I know that nothing bad will happen."

She had been on the *Keep Gen In Stone Creek* bandwagon for a few weeks and constantly tried to sell me on staying. I don't think anyone was worried that I was going to go back home to Arkansas now that Sean and the kids were leaving. Instead, I think they were concerned that I would move with Tanner and fall in love with life in a big city.

"Well, I'll have to be sure to stop by the booth so I can

watch it for you. But don't blame me if a pastry or two is missing—you can't trust me around sweets, and you already know that."

"Don't worry," she laughed. "There won't be any cream cheese danishes at the fair. I've learned to keep those *far* away from you while others are around."

My cheeks tingled when I thought about how many times Tanner and I had enjoyed the danishes recently, and I giggled when I thought of the places that they had been. Tanner was all for experimenting with food, and it turns out that other creams explode on tongues as well.

I kept my head down to hide the blush that was covering my face from the dirty thoughts I had gotten lost in.

"Are you going to see Tanner for lunch?" Brooke asked, walking behind the counter to the register.

"I'm not sure. Why?"

"He placed a lunch order, and I was going to see if you would deliver it for me?"

"Sure," I said, feeling the excitement at the thought of seeing him again.

"Cool, I'll go see if Ryder has it ready."

A few minutes later, she came out empty-handed and walked to the coffee bar on the counter behind the display case of pastries.

"It's not ready yet, but I'll get the drinks going," Brooke confirmed.

"Drinks?"

"Yeah, he ordered two pumpkin spiced lattes."

"What is it with him and those drinks?" I groaned, rolling my eyes. "It's like he lives for them."

Brooke laughed as she pressed buttons then stepped back when it started brewing.

"Hey, don't pick on him for his love of pumpkin," she teased. "Pumpkin makes people happy and more optimistic."

"Is that a scientific fact, or are you just making stuff up because you're also a pumpkin obsessed weirdo?"

"Hey—it's not just pumpkin," she corrected. "It's pumpkin *spiced*. There's a difference. And I like to think of it as pumpkin spiced possibilities because it makes you feel so happy inside that you can do anything!"

"Wow," I said sarcastically, shaking my head. Before I had time to say anything more, the door flung open, and Sheila rushed in, looking frazzled.

"Howdy, howdy, who's ready to get rowdy?" Brooke asked, using the phrase that Sheila always used.

"No—there's no time to get rowdy," Sheila said, still flustered as she tossed her purse onto the counter and looked at us. "Christmas is less than a week away, and I haven't finished my shopping."

"What's new?" Brooke laughed, earning a glare from Sheila. She pulled her lips together to keep from laughing, sensing that Sheila wouldn't find it funny.

"What's new is that I have to buy a gift for Rodney's girlfriend, and I don't know what to get her." She lifted her hands in the air in front of her and raised her brows while waiting for us to say something.

"Why do you have to get her something?" Brooke asked, frowning.

"They've been dating for over six months," she sighed heavily. "The kids love her, and honestly, I really like her too. She's been great and keeps Rodney in line, which has been really helpful these days."

I hadn't seen Rodney mad or upset that many times while we were dating, but I was there when Megan told him that she was pregnant and saw a completely different side of him. He didn't get angry or yell at her, but I swear that he looked like one of those old cartoons where he had smoke coming out of his ears and was a few seconds away from having his head pop off.

"What about a sweater or a pretty scarf?" I offered, not knowing her well enough to suggest anything more personal.

"I don't know her size, and she has sensitive skin, so I worry about getting her something that will make her itchy."

"You could always get her a nice bath set," Brooke suggested. "Maybe some candles and those little balls that you put in the tub, and they fizzle around you?"

"They don't have a tub at Rodney's house."

"Jewelry?" I threw out, knowing that it was a terrible idea. Sheila scrunched her face and shook her head no.

"Can you just come shopping and help me?" Sheila asked Brooke, batting her eyes as she pressed her hands together and begged.

Brooke eyed her suspiciously, folding her arms over her chest.

"I won't make you lock arms with me, while we skip and drink wine," Sheila muttered with a smirk. "Lucky for you, I can't have wine, so you're getting off easy with this one."

"Fine," Brooke sighed. "But I can't go until Gen gets back since Autumn is out of town, and Ryder has that meeting this afternoon with Parker and the supplier that we've been talking to."

"I'll go check on the food," I said, taking the dirty rag with me to put in the hamper in the back office.

I grabbed the order from Ryder right as he was heading out of the kitchen to bring it to Brooke.

"I added an extra sandwich," he said with a smile, handing me the brown paper bag. "I thought that you might be joining him for lunch."

"Thank you, that was very nice of you."

I felt better talking about my relationship with Ryder than I did Parker since he was more open-minded and didn't lecture me on what a big mistake I was making by dating an older man who would be leaving soon.

I grabbed the tray with the coffees from Brooke and jumped into my car, excited to see Tanner.

Once I got there, I handed Dottie the coffee that he had ordered for her. Black—no cream or sugar. Tanner joked that she liked it dark because it fed her soul, but I didn't doubt it wasn't true. She gave me the go-ahead to go to his office since I had his food order.

I was about to knock on the door when I noticed it was open a crack and he was on the phone. Just as I was about to turn and walk away, I heard something that caught my attention. I balanced the tray in my hand while gripping the bag between my fingers as I leaned closer to the door.

"Sure," he said excitedly. "I can be there January fifth."

I felt a lump in my throat as my heart fluttered at the thought of him leaving. Maybe I was wrong and had assumed that I knew what the phone call was about?

"I can't wait," he added. "It'll be nice to be back in the big city again."

I set the tray of coffee down on the floor outside of his door next to the bag of food and left. Just as I was walking out the door, I heard him calling my name behind me. I got in my car and didn't look back as I sped out of the parking lot, the tears rushing down my cheeks.

Nineteen

Tanner

I was out of breath from trying to chase after Gen's car after she flew out of the parking lot and almost got hit by a car in oncoming traffic. My heart beat wildly inside of my chest, and I wondered how much of my conversation she had heard.

I walked back inside, giving Dottie a dirty look as I stormed past her to my office. I grabbed the food and lattes from the floor and set them on my desk, running a hand through my hair in frustration. This wasn't supposed to be the way this happened. I had purposely instructed Dottie not to come back to my office while I was on the phone and assumed she understood that no one else was allowed back either.

Sitting down in the plush leather chair, I pulled out my cell phone and tried calling Gen. It went straight to voicemail again. I sent her another text message, asking her to call me. I needed to explain what happened before things got too out of control.

The stress of the day had my stomach in knots and made lunch sound unappealing. I tossed the food into the fridge, thankful that the sandwich would still be good tomorrow, so I didn't waste it. I finished the latte in record time and got started on the second one right before the next patient came in. I was already on edge and jittery, why not make it more fun with an extra caffeine boost?

By four o'clock, I still hadn't heard from Gen and knew that I wouldn't. I packed up my stuff, ready to get the hell out of there for the day. It was less than a week away from Christmas, and I was feeling the same stress that I felt every year around this time.

I took a chance and stopped by The Sweet Shop on my way home, hoping that Gen was still at work. When I walked inside, I was disappointed to see that she wasn't there as Parker and Ryder hung out behind the counter.

"Hey, Tanner," Ryder said pleasantly. "What can I help you with?"

"I was actually looking for Gen," I replied softly, feeling the heat of Parker's glare. "Have you seen her?"

"She went home early. Said she wasn't *feeling well*," Parker bit out. He hadn't bothered to move as he stared at me with his arms crossed firmly across his chest.

I nodded and turned to walk out.

"The funny thing is that she was fine this morning before she came to work," he added smugly. "Then, after she delivered your lunch, she came back feeling sick. So either

Ryder poisoned her with the sandwich he sent over for her, or you did something to upset her." He sucked in a deep breath and tilted his head slightly to the side.

"I'm sorry for bothering you guys," I said and walked toward the door. "When you see Gen, please tell her that I'm looking for her and want to talk to her."

Within seconds, Parker was across the room and closing in on me. I heard Ryder's heavy footsteps as he trailed behind him. I felt a strong hand grab my shoulder and spin me around. Parker's face was etched with anger as his nostrils flared.

"If you know what's best for you, you'll leave my daughter the fuck alone," he growled, inches away from my face as his fingers firmly dug into my skin.

"I can't do that," I admitted, looking down at the floor.

"Why not? Do you think you can just break her heart and play with her emotions? She deserves better than that, and I'll go to my grave making sure she has it."

"You don't think that I know that?!" I shouted, forcing him to let go and take a step back. Ryder's eyes widened as he waited to see what was going to happen between us.

"I know that she deserves better than me, Parker. I tell her that all the time. She doesn't listen."

"So make her."

"Have you tried to tell Gen to do something she doesn't

want to?" I asked with my eyebrow raised.

A slight smirk tried to force its way onto his face as the corners of his mouth tipped up slightly.

"No matter how hard I try, I can't walk away from her. She's like a magnet that has this hold on me that I can't break free of." I shook my head and looked away. "I tried not to fall for her, but I'm in love with her, and nothing is going to stop it."

Parker's face softened slightly when he heard me declare my love for his daughter. That didn't mean that he approved of our relationship, but maybe he understood it better now.

"Have you told her how you feel?" he asked.

I shook my head no.

"Are you going to?"

I refused to answer, knowing that I didn't have the right answer.

"Are. You. Going. To?" he asked again, enunciating each word clearly.

"No," I sighed, shoving my hands into my pockets to keep from punching something.

"Why not?"

"Because it's better for her that she doesn't know. If I tell her that I'm in love with her, then she'll feel obligated to put her life on hold to be with me, and I don't want that. I want her to be happy and to do the things that she wants to do while she's still young. Her life is just starting, and I don't want to be the reason that she puts it on hold."

Parker closed his eyes and blew out a hard breath.

"You know, you're making it really hard not to like you, Doctor Hayes," he said.

"You can call me Tanner," I teased, feeling the shift between us as the tension thinned out.

"We'll see about that."

He clapped a hand on my shoulder and winked.

<u>Twenty</u>

Gen- 5 Days Until Christmas

"I'll be back before the Winter Fair, I promise," I said loudly, hoping that the speaker in my phone wasn't cutting out again as I started to wind through the forest. The cell reception was poor, and I knew that the call was going to get dropped soon.

"I've gotta go, Sally. I'll call you tonight, okay?"

Before she could confirm, the line went dead. I tapped my fingers on the steering wheel and tried to think of anything other than Tanner while I watched the road for wildlife. The snow was thick on the ground around me, with a few icy patches on the road, but overall, the trip wasn't bad so far. It was a last-minute decision to head back to Arkansas, but I knew that I needed to do it.

I had called Sean this morning and let him know that I was headed back for a few days. The kids were excited to see me, and I had been missing them terribly. It was also the first Christmas that I hadn't celebrated at home, which was even more reason to get back before the twenty-fifth, even if I didn't stay for the actual day. I had left at five o'clock this morning, surprised by my ability to get up that early. It was a seven-hour drive which meant that I would be home mid-day and not have to do the last stretch in the dark.

Sheila and Parker were sad to see me go, but they understood where I was coming from. The holidays felt hard this year without my mom, and I was desperate to find something to fill the ache that I had in my heart from spending my first Christmas without her. I hadn't bothered to talk to Tanner before I left and figured that this was the easiest way for us to split and go our separate ways since he was leaving in a few weeks anyway.

Once I got through the thickest part of the mountain, I had better service and turned on the radio. Music was the best therapy, and I needed as much as I could get. By three o'clock, I was relieved to be pulling up to the house and back home. I felt a mix of sadness and excitement all rolled into one as I grabbed my duffle bag and got out.

I took a deep breath in and slowly let it out as I tried to prepare myself to go inside. The door flew open, and my sisters came running out to greet me. I smiled as I reached down and hugged them, knowing that I was home again. We went inside, and the smell of chili immediately made my stomach growl. Sean knew that it was my favorite comfort meal, and there was no doubt that he had made it especially for me, knowing how hard this was going to be for me.

I set my bag down in the mudroom and pulled my coat off before hanging it on the rack on the wall. The cold was still biting at my skin as I rubbed my hands together to warm up and walked into the living room.

My heart sank when I noticed that the tree wasn't up and there were no decorations anywhere in the house. It was five days until Christmas, and they still hadn't decorated? I tried to remind myself that they were grieving too and that this was just as hard for them as it was for me. Or at least half as hard.

Sean came out of the kitchen with a hand towel hung over his shoulder and a spatula in his hand.

"Hey, Gen, welcome home," he said as he wrapped an arm around to hug me.

"Thanks," I muttered, feeling completely lost. "Where's the tree and the decorations?" I asked.

"The kids didn't want to put one up this year because it reminded them too much of Amy," he said with a shrug.

"You mean their mom?" I felt the cold, icy tone slip right out of my mouth.

"Sorry, I'm used to calling her Amy."

I arched my brow, calling him on his bullshit excuse.

"She would have wanted you guys to decorate. She loved Christmas," I whispered, my throat tight as I fought to get the words out. "The tree was her favorite part."

"I know, it's just so much work, and the kids didn't seem to be that interested in it."

"Then you do it for them," I balked, surprised by how little he seemed to care.

"I haven't had the time," he sighed. "I've been busy packing stuff for the move and donating the stuff that we're not going to take."

"Donating?" My eyes widened. He had promised that I would get to go through my mom's stuff before he got rid of anything, yet everything already looked and felt different.

"Just random stuff around the house," he assured me, heading back to the kitchen. "I've left some boxes in your room with stuff for you to go through when you're up to it. Whatever you don't want, I'll add to the next donation drop-off."

I stayed in the living room, listening to the sound of the kids upstairs as music floated down and the sound of fighting came out of one of the rooms. Aside from the girls rushing out to say hi, no one seemed to care that I was home. They were busy doing whatever it was they were doing before I got here.

I tried to calm myself down, but the more I thought about everything, the angrier I got. I stormed into the kitchen and stared at Sean with my hands on my hips.

"We need to put a tree up," I insisted. "It's Christmas. The kids deserve to have a normal holiday the first year without our mom. So, we're putting the tree up."

Sean sighed and placed his hands on the counter as he hung his head.

"We can't put the tree up," he said quietly.

"Why not?"

"Because I donated it."

"You what?!" I felt like my head was going to spin off and fly into another dimension.

"I donated it after the kids said that they didn't want to put it up this year."

I covered my mouth and tried to keep the sob from escaping as my eyes filled with tears.

"We've had that tree since I was five years old. We put it up every single Christmas and decorated it as a family."

"I'm sorry, Gen. I just didn't want more to pack up and move to Alabama. I promised the kids we would get a new tree next year when we're in our new house. They were excited about it."

"This isn't about them!" I shouted, feeling myself losing control. "This is about me! I wanted that tree. It was important to me!"

I took a shaky breath, clenching and unclenching my fists at my sides.

"Where are the decorations?" I asked, my teeth gritted.

He winced as he said, "I donated those too."

I turned on my heel and stormed out of the kitchen and up the stairs to what used to be my bedroom. I slammed the door and locked it before sliding down the back of it and crying on the floor.

Twenty One

Tanner- 4 Days Until Christmas

"Another pumpkin spiced latte?" Megan asked with little enthusiasm in her tone. The only reason that I knew her name was from the first time I met her at the ultrasound, not because she had been especially friendly with me at the second appointment or any of the other times I had run into her since then.

"Actually, I was hoping to see Gen," I said, looking around, trying to find her.

"Gen's not here. Won't be back anytime soon either," she replied snidely.

"What does that mean? Did she quit?"

"No, but she went back to Arkansas. I can't say that I blame her. I would get the hell out of here the second I could if it weren't—"

"Aren't you supposed to be cleaning tables?" Parker interrupted, coming out from the kitchen. He was dressed in his usual jeans and a dark-colored fitted sweater. It matched his mood—dark and lacking color on the outside. He scowled as she rolled her eyes at him and muttered something under her breath as she walked away.

"Kids," he joked, taking her place behind the counter. "Did she get your order?"

"I actually came to see Gen," I explained again. "I really need to talk to her and haven't been able to reach her since yesterday when she came to deliver my food at the office."

"Sorry, I can't help you there. She's not talking to me either."

"Did she really go back to Arkansas?" I asked, hoping that Megan was making it up.

He nodded his head.

The bell above the door chimed, and I turned to see Brooke and Sheila walking in.

"Hey, Doc, I thought I was supposed to see you this afternoon?" Sheila asked, looking between Parker and me.

"Yeah, I just stopped by for a few minutes to talk to Gen."

"She's not here," Brooke answered, shrugging out of her coat and tossing her purse onto the table next to her before pulling off her gloves.

"So I've heard," I muttered, running a hand down my face.

"She was having a hard time with it being a few days before Christmas," Sheila explained, coming behind the counter to give Parker a quick peck on the cheek. "It was her mom's favorite time of year, and she thought that going home to where she's always celebrated the holidays would make it easier for her."

I swallowed hard, knowing that feeling all too well.

"Well, I'm glad that she's somewhere that's bringing her comfort during this hard time," I said, meaning every word. I hated that I wasn't going to get to spend Christmas with her and that I didn't know whether or not she was coming back, but I understood what she was looking for.

"That's the unfortunate part of it—she's not. When she got home yesterday, only a few of her siblings came down to greet her. The house wasn't decorated, and they didn't put the tree up. She asked her stepdad about it, and he said that he had donated it, along with the ornaments that she and her mom had collected since she was a little girl."

It felt like my heart was being shredded into a million pieces.

"You've got to be kidding me," I balked. "Who would do such a thing?"

"He insists that he didn't know that it would mean anything to her and that it was an honest mistake. She's been miserable and called me last night crying."

"Why doesn't she come home?" Parker asked, gently pushing a strand of hair out of Sheila's face.

"She's feeling lost right now. She doesn't know where she belongs and is desperately trying to find something that feels normal in this new world that she's been forced to live in. Her mom was the only constant that she's ever had in her life, and now she's gone. Gen just needs some time to heal and take that first step forward. It'll be hard, but we'll be there for her every step of the way."

"Sheila, I'm sorry, but I need to cancel our appointment today," I blurted out suddenly. There were a million thoughts running through my head, and I had a lot that I needed to get done in a short period.

"Oh, okay," she replied, taken aback. "Is everything okay?"

"No, but it will be. There's something that I need to do."

"Is there anything that we can do to help?"

"Yeah, can you point me in the right direction to Arkansas?"

Twenty Two

Gen- Four Days Until Christmas

"I know that I promised, Sally," I said softly, hating that she was crying on the other line. "I'm still going to try to make it back for the Winter Fair if I can."

"But it's in *two days*. Mom said that you might spend Christmas in Arkansas with your other family."

"I haven't figured out what I'm doing yet. Things are really hard for me right now."

"I know, I'm sorry," she sighed, and I was glad that she didn't have any idea what I was going through, even though she was trying to relate to me.

"If I don't make it back," I sucked in a deep breath and tried to force the words out, knowing that I had already broken my promise to her and that I wouldn't be back in time. "I will make it up to you. Okay?"

"Alright."

"Can I talk to your mom?"

I knew that I needed to fill Sheila in on our conversation so she would understand why Sally was in such a bad mood—other than she was a hormonal teenager who hated the world most days lately.

"She's not here."

I pulled my head back, surprised. It was Friday afternoon, and Sheila was always off from her job early. On top of that, they usually gave her the days leading up to Christmas off to spend time with her family. The holiday fell on a Monday this year, so I imagined that she would have been off today.

"Where is she?"

"I don't know. She and Parker left earlier for some secret something or another. All that I know is that Megan and Oliver are in charge until my dad and Lizzie come to pick us up."

"Oh, well, maybe they're just out running errands and finishing up their shopping," I suggested, remembering how stressed Sheila was yesterday about not being done yet.

"Who knows," Sally muttered, not having the same amount of interest in it as I did.

"Well, if you need anything, just call me."

"I'll be fine," she sighed, the teenager in her coming out again. "I'm not a kid, and I'll be stuck at my dad's house anyway."

"Alright, well, I'll talk to you soon."

I ended the call and laid down on the bed. Deep down, I was more hurt with Sean than I was angry, but since no one seemed bothered that I didn't come out of my room to spend time with them, I hadn't made much of an effort.

Instead of going through my mom's stuff and letting Sean donate what I didn't want, I had loaded up the trunk of my car and packed it so full that it barely closed. I'd decided that I wasn't going to get rid of anything until I decided that I was ready, even if it meant that I had to find someplace to store it until then.

I had taken the time while he was out with the kids earlier and walked through the house, hoping to feel her in it still. I closed my eyes and sat on the couch where she used to braid my hair as a teenager before I would spend hours at the creek with my friends. I remembered the way her fingers felt as she maneuvered my hair effortlessly into a fishtail braid or whatever crazy concoction that I had wanted that day. She never complained about it, just sat on the couch and listened to me talk about whatever teenage drama I had going on at the time while she did my hair.

Being alone in the house was helpful, and I found that I could still feel her stronger in certain parts than others. Most of what I had left was from the memories that I had been cherishing inside my head and not from the few things that were left that hadn't been packed up yet. I browsed the photos on the mantle above the fireplace and took the ones that were my favorite, leaving Sean the ones that had him or the kids in them. I doubted that he would even notice the others were missing—like the one of my mom and dad, holding me a few days after I was born. It was the only picture that I had of the three of us, and I was damned if I wasn't going to be the one to keep it.

The day was getting late, and I knew that soon the house would be full again and that I wouldn't have any more time to myself. I took what I could and made peace knowing that this would never be home again, and that was okay. When I thought about home, I started to picture Stone Creek and the family that I had gotten closer to there.

I was still lying on my bed when I heard car doors close. I pulled the pillow over my head and grumbled, not ready to see or deal with anyone yet. My heart was still in a fragile state, and I couldn't bear any more sadness or disappointment tonight. I got up and made an effort to go downstairs to greet them, knowing that I needed to spend some time with them before I left to go back to Stone Creek, and they moved to Alabama. It felt weird how easy it was now to decide that I was going *home*.

As I got to the last stair, there was a knock on the door. I walked over and rolled my eyes as I pulled it open.

"Did you forget your keys again?" I teased, knowing that Sean and the kids were lazy enough to knock instead of bothering to unlock the door themselves. Only, it wasn't Sean or the kids.

I recognized the spicy fragrance of his cologne before I saw him, the pull of my body to his as strong as it always was. My mouth suddenly went dry, and I couldn't get any words out.

"Can I come in?" he asked, shivering in the cold even though he was bundled up.

"Um, yeah," I said slowly, still unable to believe that he was there. I stepped back and held the door open for him to come inside.

"Us too?" Sheila asked as she and Parker came around the giant bush that lined the sidewalk to the door.

My eyes almost popped out of my head as I watched them walk through the door behind Tanner.

"What are you guys doing here?" I closed the door quickly, shutting out the cold before it could come in and ruin this perfect daydream that I was having.

"Tanner had something that he needed to say to you," Parker said smoothly, sitting down on the couch.

"You can't just make yourself at home," Sheila scolded, standing next to him.

"No one's here," I interjected, glancing from Tanner, who was standing in front of me, to them. "Besides, it would be fine if they were."

I turned my attention back to Tanner and noticed his Adam's apple bob as he swallowed down his nerves.

"Gen, I'm sorry to just barge in here without asking, but I have something to say to you that couldn't wait."

"Okay," I whispered, still trying to wrap my head around the fact that he was here—in my house—well, technically my *old* house.

"I am head over heels in love with you, Gen. I can't stop thinking about you, and when you're not around, I feel like my days are dark and dull. You're the light that brightens the room when you walk in, and you're the only person that I've ever felt so comfortable opening up to. I know that you're trying to find the next path in your life, but I needed you to know that I need you in mine. So, whatever decision you make, I hope you'll consider making one that allows me to stay in your life."

He paused for a moment and glanced over his shoulder at Parker. Something had definitely changed between them, besides that Parker was being nice and not shooting daggers at him with his eyes. My dad nodded, and Tanner turned back to me and continued.

"If you want to live in Arkansas, I'll find a clinic to work at out here. If you want to go to Alabama, I'll follow you there. There are endless options for work, Gen, but only one true love, and that's you."

The tears slid down my cheeks faster than I could stop them. My throat burned, and my eyes blurred as I struggled to find the words to say.

"Tanner, I know about you taking the other job."

I bit my tongue to try to keep the tears back as my lower lip trembled.

"What other job?"

"The one that you start in the *big city* on January fifth. I heard you on the phone and heard all about it."

"Gen, that wasn't what you thought it was."

I wrapped my arms around my middle protectively. How could he sit there and tell me that I was wrong when I knew what I had heard?

"I was standing right there. You said it yourself."

He took a step toward me, a mischievous smile on his face.

"I know what I said."

I was starting to feel frustrated and hated not knowing what was going on. Sheila and Parker sat there quietly, not bothering to jump in and help.

"Okay, then what exactly is going on?" I demanded, angrier than I had expected.

"I was planning a trip," he said vaguely.

"A trip?"

He nodded.

"I take one every year right after New Year's, so I can be gone on January seventh."

"Why?"

My anger was slowly starting to fade as my curiosity piqued.

"Because," he breathed heavily, reaching out to hold both of my hands. "I lost my mother on January seventh."

His words plunged through my heart, twisting inside the wound that was already open and oozing.

"I have a little sister, Emily, that I take with me. She's fifteen now but still loves when we take trips together. She doesn't know why we go in January, and I hope that she never remembers."

"Was she young when your mom died?"

"It happened a few years ago, but she has Down's Syndrome and doesn't remember *when* it happened. It's hard enough that she knows that my mom is gone, but I always feel this responsibility to distract her—us, on the anniversary of when it happened. Just in case she starts to remember. I don't want her to feel that pain and my theory has always been that she can't feel the pain if we're out having fun."

I didn't bother wiping the tears away as he shared this intimate story of his life with me. We were so similar in so many ways that I now understood why he got me better than anyone I'd ever met.

"When you heard me on the phone, I was talking to my other sister and planning a trip for all of us at Disneyland."

I lowered my eyes in embarrassment.

"I'm so sorry," I apologized. "I just heard you talking about a date and the big city and assumed that you were taking a new job after we had talked about your contract ending at the end of this month."

"It's okay," he smiled, reaching for my hands again now that I was done wiping tears away. "I've been trying to find you so I could explain, but you've been a little hard to track down."

"I know, I'm sorry that I didn't give anyone much notice before I left. I thought that coming back would help me find what I was looking for and help me through the holidays without my mom, but it just left me feeling emptier and more alone."

"I think we have something that can fix that," Tanner said, his cheeks splitting as the smile stretched across his face and showed off his perfect white teeth. "Come with me," he insisted, pulling me toward the door. Sheila and Parker got up and followed us outside.

Parked in the street, in front of the house, was Sheila's SUV. I heard the click as it was unlocked before Tanner opened the back door.

I gasped and covered my mouth as I stared inside.

"You found it?!" I asked emotionally, my voice cracking at the end.

"We went by several shops in town until we found the one that Sean had donated it to," Parker explained. "We would have been here sooner, but Sheila saw a few things that she just *had to have*," he teased.

"Hey, I was finishing my Christmas shopping," she insisted. "We are four days away, and you're still not done, mister." She wagged her finger at him playfully.

"I can't believe that you went and bought my old tree. That's the sweetest thing that anyone has ever done for me, you guys."

"We knew how much it meant to you," Sheila said softly, rubbing her hand across my back.

"It was Tanner's idea," Parker added. "He was coming here to get it, with or without us."

"That means so much to me, thank you," I cried, my face raw from the saltiness of my tears.

"There's more," Tanner said, gently leading me to the back of the SUV. He pressed the button to open the trunk, and I looked inside. My eyes widened, and I turned to look at him.

"You bought all of the ornaments too?"

"Actually, no," he said softly. "When I explained what had happened, the guy just gave them to me. It turns out that he knew your mother and used to teach her piano when she was a little girl."

"Mr. King," I smiled, knowing exactly who he was talking about. "He's one of the nicest people that I've ever met."

"He said the same about you. In addition to giving us the tree and the ornaments, he also added a new one for you to add to your collection."

Tanner reached inside and pulled out a small brown paper bag. My fingers trembled as I took it and carefully pulled out the box inside. He took the bag from me and smiled while I opened it.

Inside was a beautiful white ceramic angel with wings that were paper thin and sheer. Her hands were pulled close to her chest as she held a small red heart inside them.

"Look at the bottom," Tanner suggested.

I gently tipped her over, making sure that my grip on her was tight enough to keep me from dropping it while soft enough not to break anything.

On the bottom, in a fine ink, were the words: home is always where the heart is.

I turned my head and tried to keep the sob from escaping my throat as Tanner wrapped me in his arms and held me.

"I know that you've felt lost and like you haven't found your way," he whispered. "But we're here for you, Gen. Just tell us what you need, and we'll take care of you."

"I can't believe you guys came all the way down here and did all of this for me," I whimpered.

"You're our family," Sheila reminded me. "We will always be wherever you need us. Nothing will ever change that."

The past few days, I had felt so down and alone, and not even fifteen minutes with them, I felt like I belonged. I was happy and felt wanted.

"It's getting too cold for my liking," Parker complained, rubbing his hands together. "Just tell us where you want the tree, and we'll help you put it up and decorate it."

"I want to take it home," I said proudly, looking up at the house behind us.

"Okay, I'll start unpacking the ornaments first," Parker confirmed, moving toward us.

"No," I breathed, finally feeling like I could take a deep breath. "I want to go home. To Stone Creek, where I belong."

Twenty Three

Tanner- 3 Days Until Christmas

"Where do you want to put it?" I asked Gen once we finished unpacking the tree and decorations from the SUV. Parker and I were exhausted from driving to Arkansas and then back with little rest in between. We were able to tow Gen's Corolla back with Sheila's Tahoe, which allowed us to all ride back together after we moved the tree to Gen's car to make more room. We rested while the girls took turns driving back to Stone Creek and talking, but I still felt like I needed another ten hours of sleep to feel back to normal.

"Can we put it over there, by the window?" she asked nervously, pointing while chewing a nail on her other hand.

"It can go anywhere you want it," I smiled, leaning in to kiss her on the cheek.

It felt wonderful to have Gen back at my house, and the stack of boxes in the corner of the living room didn't bother me either. It was all of the stuff that she had packed up and brought back with her from Arkansas that she was trying to store in her car until she figured out where she was going to live.

Parker and Sheila had the room for now, but when the new babies came, they would need to spread out, which meant that Megan would need her own room again. I offered Gen to stay with me as long as she wanted and had to convince her to move her stuff out of her car. Before Gen left for Arkansas, I had felt torn on whether or not I wanted to continue my contract in Stone Creek or move somewhere else. But now that I knew what it felt like to be without her, I didn't want to let her go ever again.

"Thank you," she whispered, the tears swelling in her eyes again as she stared at the tree in front of the window where the snow was falling outside.

"You don't have to thank me." I wiped the tear from her cheek with my thumb and wrapped a hand around her waist. She leaned into me and rested her head against my chest.

"It means so much to me that you went through all of this effort for me. I know that it's silly because it's just a tree, but—"

"Gen, it's not silly. It's special, and that makes it important. Don't ever apologize for how you're feeling. I'm glad that we were able to help get the tree and decorations back for you."

"Me too. It's not the same as spending Christmas with her, but I feel like she's still here with me," she choked out.

"She is," I whispered, feeling the tightness in my throat.

We spent the afternoon decorating the tree and drinking wine, laughing at my failed attempt to get the star on the tree at the perfect angle and ended the night wrapped in each other's arms. If I ever wondered whether or not small-town life was for me, I found my answer every time I looked into her beautiful, green eyes. I would go to the ends of the earth to be with her.

Twenty Four

Gen- 2 Days Until Christmas

"Over there is where they have the face painting booth, and then around the corner is where Mr. Gianni has the *best* caramel apples!" Sally shrieked, pulling me by one hand while Tanner held the other.

I don't know what she was more excited about—the Winter Fair itself or being able to show me around. Well, technically, *us* since Tanner had never been to one either.

"This is amazing," I said happily, taking in the sights around me. There were booths set up along both sides of Main Street, which had been blocked off hours ago as they started setting up for the fair. Each booth was decked out in beautiful white Christmas lights, creating the illusion of houses stacked along the street. The trees on the sidewalk had been lit up as well, but the real sight to see was the forty-five foot Christmas tree in the middle of the street where the carolers were gathered, singing Silent Night.

"You definitely don't see anything like this in the big city," Tanner mumbled, looking around in awe. "Or at least, I never have. They have big events that I've been to, but they don't have *this* vibe."

I nodded, knowing what he was talking about. I felt it too and found it hard to describe because I hadn't felt anything like this before either.

"I'm gonna go find my mom and Parker. I'll catch up with you later," Sally said before she ran off.

"Will she be okay on her own?" Tanner asked, looking over his shoulder to watch where she went.

"Yeah, I see Parker over there." I nodded to where he was standing by Brooke and Ryder's booth, his eyes fixated on Sally as she wandered around on her way to them.

We walked around, holding hands, and enjoying the festivities together. After a bit, we sat down for dinner and enjoyed a warm bowl of soup with freshly baked bread that was to die for. Even though I wasn't in Arkansas and didn't have my mom with me, I was starting to feel the Christmas spirit around me.

After a while, we met up with Sheila, Parker, and the kids, which was a hard enough feat, getting everyone in one place at one time. I knew that it wasn't a coincidence, but when the kids were grinning from ear to ear, I knew that something was up.

"What's going on?" I asked, looking between everyone, waiting for an answer.

"You'll find out in just a few minutes," Sheila said lightly, her eyes sparkling with happiness.

A few minutes later, Brooke and Ryder came rushing over, pulling their coats tighter against them.

"Alright, we're here!" Brooke exclaimed, her smile matching the others. Ryder gave me a quick hug and kissed the top of my head, making me even more suspicious.

"Okay, let's get going then," Parker said, clapping his hands. He started walking toward the massive Christmas tree with everyone following behind him.

"What's happening?" I whispered to Brooke, who was walking beside me.

"You'll see," she laughed, knowing better than to tell me what was going on.

I started to feel the excitement build up inside of me and wondered if Tanner was in on whatever this was as well. He didn't look at me as I glanced up at him, just squeezed my hand and kept walking.

A few minutes later, we were lined up to see Santa, and I felt the laughter starting to bubble over.

"You brought me to see Santa?" I asked, giggling.

"Yes and no," Parker laughed. "I mean, it's up to you if you want to tell him what you want for Christmas. I won't stop you."

We took a few steps forward until the girl dressed as an elf called us over and told us where to stand around Santa. There was a large backdrop behind us that had been built to look like the north pole. A jolly-looking man sat in the oversized plush white chair, waiting for us to get situated. The elves sat the kids in front of Santa while the adults stood beside him, Ryder and Brooke on one side and Sheila and Parker on the other.

I wasn't sure where to go, so I just stood there, feeling like I didn't have a place that I belonged. I wasn't one of the kids, so it felt weird to sit in front with them, but I also didn't fit in with the other adults. I swallowed hard, fighting down the panic that I started to feel from being the odd one out.

"Okay, follow me this way, miss," the older elf said. I took their lead and accepted their hand as they helped me up to where Santa was sitting without stepping on any of the kids along the way.

"You can sit on the arm of the chair," the other elf noted, pointing to the wide space with plenty of room for me to sit.

I noticed that Tanner was still standing off to the side and hated that he wasn't included. I was about to get down and go over to him when Parker spoke up.

"We have one more person," he said, pointing to Tanner. "My future son-in-law needs to be in our first family picture."

I whipped my head back and looked at him, unsure that I had heard him correctly.

When I turned around again, Tanner was standing beside

me, kneeling on one knee with a ring box in his hand. I covered my mouth, trying to force the tears away.

"Tanner!" I exclaimed.

"Gen, I know that you and I haven't been dating very long, but I've gotten a glimpse at what my life would be like without you, and I don't ever want to feel that way again. You're the sunshine that brightens my darkest days. You're the beauty that colors the world around you and makes it a better place to be. And most of all, you're the sweetest, most genuine person that I've ever met, and I would be so honored to spend the rest of my life trying to be the man that you deserve. Will you marry me?"

I heard the gasps and oohs whispered around me as the tears flowed down my face. I jumped up off of the chair and knelt in front of Tanner, holding his face in my hands as I kissed him.

"Yes, Tanner, I'll marry you!"

We stood up, and he slipped the most beautiful antique ring on my finger. I stared at it for so long that I forgot anyone else was around us.

"It's beautiful," I whispered.

"It was my mom's. I promised her that I would give it to the woman I would spend forever with."

"I love you so much, Tanner."

He pulled me in closer for a kiss that took my breath away.

"Um, I hate to interrupt this sweet moment, but can we do the family photo?" Parker asked playfully.

"Yes, yes!" I laughed, taking Tanner's hand as he helped me back up to the side of the chair. He took his place on the other arm, and soon, we were all saying cheese and taking our first official family photo.

I thought that I lost my family when my mother died, but little did I know that I had another one waiting to love me as much as she had.

Epilogue

Gen- Six Months Later

"Happy Father's Day," I said as I hugged Parker.

"Thank you for making me a father," he whispered, hugging me tighter.

Our relationship had changed so much over the past six months that I lived in Stone Creek. It helped that we had dinner together as a family a few times a week and that Sheila and I talked every day. I never imagined that I would have another woman that I was as close to as I was with my mom, but somehow I was lucky enough to have that with Sheila.

"Can I help with anything?" I asked, walking into the kitchen where Sheila was standing at the stove, boiling corn on the cob. Her hair was piled up on her head into a giant ball of red frizzy hair, the heat and humidity adding to the curliness.

"Ugh," she groaned, looking over her shoulder. "I am too pregnant to be standing at this hot stove. I've got an oven inside of me, I don't need anything else to make me hotter."

"Here, why don't I take over that for you?" I offered, gently grabbing her shoulders and turning her away as I took the tongs from her hand.

"You're a doll, thank you."

I gave her belly a quick rub to say hello to the baby and began turning the rest of the corn in the pot. I wasn't sure how long they needed to boil, but I was desperate for something to keep my mind busy. I had practiced what I was going to say all day, but yet I still couldn't find the courage to spit it out.

Tanner was outside at the grill with Parker while the kids helped set the table under the tree in the shade. Sheila had also instructed them to put as many fans outside as possible to help cool it off some.

"How much longer does it need to boil?" I asked, turning to find Sheila bent over, her fingers clutching the table as she sat on the edge of the chair.

"Sheila? Are you okay?" I quickly turned off the stove and moved the pot to the back burner when I saw the puddle beneath her. She was breathing heavily, her eyes squinted closed in pain. "Oh my God, you're not due for three more weeks!"

"I know," she gritted out.

I turned and opened the backdoor, looking for Tanner, hoping he was still close by. I groaned when I didn't see him, knowing that I would have to leave Sheila for a minute to find him. I let the door close behind me as I ran outside, finding him by the shed in the back.

"Tanner! Tanner!" I called, the panic in my voice enough to get his attention. Parker's face fell, and they both took off running toward me.

"What happened?" Tanner asked when he was close enough for me to hear him.

"Sheila is in labor," I breathed, running back with them. Why was their backyard so freaking big?

We all rushed back in and found Sheila standing at the table, holding onto the back of the chair as she cried out in pain. She had on a loose, flowy summer dress that was now stained from where she had been sitting when her water broke.

"Are you having contractions?" Tanner asked, rushing to get to Sheila. He quickly assessed her before yelling over his shoulder to Parker. "Grab me some towels and a blanket! Gen, rush out to the car and grab my bag!"

Parker took off down the hallway while I rushed out to get what he needed.

A few minutes later, I was back inside, setting the bag down beside him. He wasted no time opening it and grabbing a clean pair of gloves. He slid them on and lifted Sheila's dress out of the way.

"Okay, Sheila. You are completely dilated, and I can see the baby's head. On your next contraction, I want you to push as hard as you can. Okay?"

She nodded, panting as Parker stood behind her and helped to hold her. I stood off to the side, out of the way. I didn't know whether I should leave and give her some privacy, but then I also didn't want to go far in case Tanner needed something.

Sheila started grunting again as another contraction started.

"Push," Tanner said as Parker held her dress out of the way. She cried out as she pushed harder, her legs shaking beneath her. "Don't let her fall. These next few pushes are going to be intense as she pushes the baby out."

Parker nodded and kept his grip around her waist, planting a kiss on the top of her head.

"Okay, Sheila, you're doing great. I need you to push even harder with the next contraction, okay?"

She cried harder as her scream echoed through the kitchen.

"Perfect! Her head is out, but you need to keep pushing for me. On three, I want you to push again. Ready? One. Two. Three. Push!"

I covered my mouth as I watched the baby's tiny body come out as Tanner masterfully delivered it and wrapped it in one of the clean towels that Parker had brought out.

"Okay, let her sit down," Tanner said to Parker. Slowly, he eased her onto the chair after I rushed over and put a towel down for her to sit on. It wasn't much, but I imagined it would be softer than the chair.

"Here's your beautiful baby girl," Tanner whispered, carefully handing the baby to Sheila. Parker hugged her from behind and bent down to see his daughter. I wiped the tears from my eyes and smiled. It was one of the most beautiful things that I had ever seen.

I stepped out to give them some privacy while Tanner finished up. The kids would be excited to meet their new sibling but definitely didn't need to see any of that right now. Besides, I imagined that Sheila would want some privacy before her kids came in and saw her fully exposed.

Thirty minutes later, I was sitting at the back table while Thomas and Oliver took over grilling the food that Parker and Tanner had started before Sheila went into labor. Brooke and Ryder pulled up out front and made their way out to the back before going inside. I had texted her to let her know that Sheila was in labor and that I would update her as I knew more.

"Did she have the baby?" Brooke asked as she rushed over to where I was sitting.

"She did," I sighed, remembering the moment that she was born. "I haven't seen them since then, though."

"I'm sure they're just getting her situated and cleaning stuff up," Brooke said quietly. I chuckled, knowing how much Ryder had been nervous about all of the new babies coming soon.

"There was a lot to clean up," I laughed, remembering the mess that was still there before I came outside.

"Does it make you think twice about having kids?" she asked with a smile.

"Na, I think I'll be just fine."

I felt my cheeks burn after I said it, wondering if anyone else had heard my slip.

Just then, the back door opened, and Tanner came out. He was grinning from ear to ear.

"Hey, guys," he said as he came over to hug Ryder and Brooke.

"How's Sheila and the baby?" Ryder asked.

"They're both doing great," he said, sitting down beside me and wrapping an arm around me. "They'll be out in a few minutes."

"We can go inside if it's too much for her. I don't want to stress her with moving around too much," I said nervously.

"She'll be okay, trust me. I could barely keep her in the chair long enough to deliver the placenta," he joked.

Ryder's face paled, and he looked away.

The back door opened again, and Sheila walked out, holding the baby wrapped tightly in a clean receiving blanket. Parker was right behind her, one hand on her waist as he helped her down the two stairs outside.

"Hey, everyone," Sheila said, sounding tired.

Ryder whistled and got the attention of Megan and Sally, who were off sitting at the other table across the yard. They got up and came over to join us as Thomas and Oliver closed the lid on the grill and stood beside Ryder.

"We would like you guys to meet Layla Mae Hudson," Sheila announced, gently rubbing the baby's cheek with her finger.

"She's beautiful," I whispered as she held her out for me to see, making her way around to everyone.

I felt Tanner's hand tighten around my waist as he hugged me, knowing the secret that I was still keeping from my family.

After Sheila had taken the baby around to meet everyone, she sat down in the plush chair that Parker insisted on bringing outside and nursed the baby. The guys plated the meat while Brooke and I got the food from inside prepared and brought it out to the table. As everyone was sitting down to eat, Parker stood at the end of the table by Sheila and watched her with his baby.

It melted my heart to see how much he loved them. And now that I had Tanner, I understood what that love was like. It was different than anything I had ever felt before. As Parker sat down, I stood up, suddenly feeling like my legs were going to give out. Tanner stood up beside me, squeezing my hand encouragingly.

"Before we get started, I have something that I would like to say," I announced nervously.

Everyone stopped what they were doing—except for the baby, she was going to town and didn't look like she would stop any time soon—and gave me their attention. I cleared my throat and pulled in a deep breath.

"This time last year, I was struggling with my mom's illness and didn't know then how much my life would change within a year. After she died, I felt lost and couldn't find my way. The last words that my mom said to me were that she wanted me to live life and be happy. For the longest time, I thought that there was some hidden meaning in that. Maybe she wanted me to travel the world and have all of these crazy adventures. Or perhaps she just wanted me to be happy. Either way, I keep those words close to my heart every single day. I make sure that whatever I'm doing, it brings me happiness.

"In a few months, I will marry the love of my life, and I can't wait to start that chapter with him. I have a family that I love and adore, and I don't know what I would do without you guys. Each one of you is so incredibly special to me, and I will never be able to tell you how much you mean to me."

I paused and took a deep breath, my fingers shaking at my sides.

"Family is important to me, and that's why Tanner and I are happy to announce that we're growing our family."

He pulled me into his side and whispered in my ear, "I love you."

"You're pregnant?!" Sheila asked excitedly, startling the baby.

"Yes," I laughed. "I'm due November twenty-third."

"Aww, a little pumpkin spiced baby!" Brooke exclaimed, clapping her hands.

"Like you said, pumpkin-spiced possibilities," I laughed, feeling my heart grow bigger with how excited my family was for our new baby.

I looked up at Tanner, the man who came into my life when I didn't know how much I needed him. My life felt like it was spinning out of control, but he ended up being the rock that helped ground me. We both knew the pain of losing a parent and carried that grief with us daily, but when we worked as a team, that grief was bearable, and our love outshined our darkest days.

****
****

Thank you so much for reading Gen and Tanner's story! I hope you've enjoyed the charming town of Stone Creek!

If you're curious to see what happened at Disneyland when Tanner took his sister, be sure to grab this newsletter exclusive, Caramel Dipped Adventures!

https://storyoriginapp.com/giveaways/6c216fb8-3b53-11ec-9721-4b6593099ce4

If you're looking for more small-town romance but want more action and thrill, be sure to check out my Haven Brook series! It's romantic suspense packed with plenty of heat!

'Til Death Do Us Part (Haven Brook Book 1) https://books2read.com/u/m2RJNR

Looking for something that will tug at your heart and take you on a wild ride? Check out my sweet romance, One Last Wish! https://books2read.com/u/mqg7D9

184

Other Books By Samantha Baca

The Haven Brook Series:

'Til Death Do Us Part (Haven Brook Book 1)

https://books2read.com/u/m2RJNR

The Cradle Will Fall (Haven Brook Book 2)

https://books2read.com/u/b6O0QE

The Ties That Bind (Haven Brook Book 3)

https://books2read.com/u/mqgoz8

A Very Haven Christmas (Haven Brook Book 4- Novella)

https://books2read.com/u/mvqGjj

Three Strikes, You're Gone (Haven Brook Book 5)

https://books2read.com/u/mvqL2z

The Dark Shadows Series

Five Steps Ahead (Dark Shadows Book 1)

https://books2read.com/u/38Q0gO

Ten Seconds Too Late (Dark Shadows Book 2)

Coming 2022

Against The Clock (Dark Shadows Book 3)

Coming 2023

Out Of Time (Dark Shadows Book 4)

Coming 2023

The Stone Creek Series (Novellas)

Chocolate Covered Mistletoe (Stone Creek Book 1)

https://books2read.com/u/3LRk9N

Candy Coated Promises (Stone Creek Book 2)

https://books2read.com/u/mldP5Y

Pumpkin Spiced Possibilities (Stone Creek Book 3)

https://books2read.com/u/bojdwV

<u>Standalone Books</u>

One Last Wish

https://books2read.com/u/mqg7D9

Finding Love In Apartment 2C (Novella)

https://books2read.com/u/bze9aZ

Cocky Counsel: A Hero Club Novel

https://bit.ly/CockyCounsel

<u>Holiday Books</u>

Snow Place To Go

https://books2read.com/u/4A560N

A Christmas Wish (coming 12/1/2021)

https://books2read.com/u/4EKXpE

<u>Acknowledgements</u>

First and foremost, thank you to all of the readers who have picked up a copy of this book! Thank you so much for your support and for choosing my book to read out of the thousands of options available to you. I hope that you're able to get lost in these wonderful worlds that I've created and that you walk away feeling happier to have read this story.

As always, I owe a huge amount of gratitude to my alpha readers, Azucena and Chelsea. Without you ladies these books wouldn't be what they are. I love your support and enthusiasm every time I come to you with a new idea. Thank you for picking me up when I'm feeling down and pushing me to keep writing. I love you ladies so much!

I also have the most amazing beta readers and couldn't imagine working through a book without them. Katy, Camille, and Amanda—your feedback is so valuable to me and I'm so thankful that you take the time out of your busy schedules to help me!

Tillie—you constantly amaze me with meeting deadlines for editing when you have so much going on! Thank you for always making me a priority and helping me with these stinking edits. You're the best!

Richard—you are the best husband, editor, cover creator, proofreader, father, and everything else that I could ever ask for. I'm pretty sure you're a genie because you seem to be able to make all of my wishes come true. And I wouldn't be a romance author without a corny line or two, right? Thank you for everything you do for me, I appreciate you so much.

Thank you to my parents and sister for always being there, cheering for me to keep pushing books out into the world. I love your enthusiasm and support! You make the impossible feel like it's possible and I'm so thankful for that.

To my sweet girls—sometimes in life, things get hard and it's easy to want to give up. Let this book be proof that you can do anything if you just keep trying. The things that are harder to do end up being the most satisfying once we're done. I love you both and can't wait to see what dreams you chase after.

If you've enjoyed this book, please consider dropping by Goodreads or BookBub to let others know! You can also follow me on both platforms to stay up to date when I have a new release.

About the Author

Samantha lives in the southwest with her husband and two small children after abandoning her childhood dream of living in a cabin in Colorado when she found that she couldn't afford to live there and was deathly allergic to the woods. When she's not writing she's usually spouting off sarcastic remarks while drinking wine out of a coffee mug to look like a functional adult while chasing down her toddlers. She enjoys spending time with her family, watching reruns of Friends, and the 24/7 flow of coffee that can be found in her veins. Be sure to follow her on social media for updates on what she's working on.

You can find her here:
Facebook: https://www.facebook.com/AuthorSamanthaBaca
Instagram: https://instagram.com/author_samantha_baca
Goodreads: http://www.goodreads.com/authorsamanthabaca
Facebook Reader Group: https://www.facebook.com/
groups/2945710968775398/
Webpage: https://authorsamanthabaca.wordpress.com
Newsletter: http://eepurl.com/g0NcSj

www.ingramcontent.com/pod-product-compliance
Lightning Source LLC
Chambersburg PA
CBHW061535310726
48972CB00008B/2463